WELCOME TO MEADOWBROOK

CASSANDRA L. THOMPSON

Welcome to Meadowbrook
written by Cassandra L. Thompson
published by Quill & Crow Publishing House

Edited by Lisa Morris, Mathew L. Reyes

Cover Design by Fay Lane

Printed in the United States of America

ISBN (ebook): 978-1-958228-62-3

ISBN (paperback): 978-1-958228-63-0

Publisher's Website: quillandcrowpublishinghouse.com

For Andrew, my partner in time

Something about old hotels. The way the ghosts of a hundred different stories linger in the halls. The smell of sanitized sheets that can't compete with the musty aroma of age. A liminal space where you don't have to exist. Or you can. Either way, you'll be forgotten.

— POEM, CASSANDRA L. THOMPSON

This book contains themes of death, violence, and abuse.
Please be sure to consult the Trigger Index at the back of
the book for more information.

PREFACE

Dearest Reader,

And so we meet again.

I'm thrilled you've decided to give *Welcome to Meadowbrook* a whirl. After a few years of writing gothic, romantic vampires, I needed to cleanse my palate a little. If you follow me on my many social media platforms, you probably have figured out by now that my husband and I love to travel. We've discovered plenty of hotels along the way, and I find myself regularly inspired by them—especially the older ones. There is something so liminal and eerie about a building full of rooms that have seen hundreds, if not thousands, of people in and out of them. Each person with their own story, adding to the story of the hotel itself. And don't even get me started on elevators. This is what gave me the idea to write *Meadowbrook*; I wanted to write a story of stories.

Fans of haunted places and infamous ghost tours might recognize all the Crescent Hotel "Easter eggs" I've woven into the story. Though the Crescent was a huge inspiration for the Meadowbrook Hotel, I wanted to write my own story. I did, however, incorporate some interesting pieces of the Crescent's history with a Cassandra twist. If you want to learn more about the actual history of the

Crescent Hotel—which is fascinating in its own right—be sure to research it online. Meadowbrook is her own story, however, and I hope you will find it as enjoyable as I did writing it.

Welcome to Meadowbrook is structured in a way that you can read the novel forward or backward, though I recommend reading it straight on first. As always, please be sure to check the trigger warnings. They are indexed in the back of the book. Also, if you are the type of reader who hates ambiguity and filling in narrative blanks with your imagination, this is probably not the book for you.

And that's enough from me, dearest reader. Enjoy your stay.

Dreadfully Yours,
Cassandra L. Thompson

PROLOGUE

Theodora, 1938

"Cancer is not real." His voice crackled over the radio. "It's a fallacy created by charlatans who want to bleed you dry of your hard-earned cash. That is why they all hate me! The American Medical Association is full of failures, and guess what?" The tinny sound was joined by others, chanting in unison: *"If you can cure after others fail, you're a quack!"*

In the last burst of energy I would ever have, I threw my water glass across the room. It hit the radio and shattered, silencing the voice I'd heard for hours every morning. For how many days, weeks, months, I could not tell you.

A nurse burst into the room. "Is everything alright?"

"I can hear him speak no longer!" I sputtered, shocked by my own candor. "When will he fix my arm?"

Her eyes were hard, though she feigned kindness and concern in her expression. She gingerly lifted the foul, sopping bandage from the soft part of my arm, trying not to wince at my wound. Painful bubbles of yellow pus had grown along the site where they'd administered injections intended to cure me. They'd given me drugstore pills for the fever and poured alcohol on the open wounds, but with each new treatment, the infection got worse. A part of me knew I needed real medical care, but this was not a hospital. It was *better* than a hospital.

"We'll have to lance it again," she sighed.

"Is that why I'm not getting better?" I asked.

"You'll have to talk to Doc." She marched over to the radio and turned the dial a few times. When she realized I'd silenced his voice forever, she withdrew without another word.

No one came back in for a full day. My fever spiked, and I couldn't get up from the bed. I'm deeply ashamed to admit I soiled myself, but I was too weak to call for help. I assumed I was being punished for the radio incident.

In the middle of the night, they came.

Two men lifted me from my soiled sheet and put me on a gurney. I was too weak to be modest, letting them manhandle me without objection. My rising fever burned behind my eyes, causing my vision to waver as they quietly wheeled me down the carpeted halls.

I didn't start to panic until I heard the moaning.

My eyes shot open, fear sharpening my focus. I was in a wing I'd never seen before. Gone was the whimsical wallpaper and the cheerful paint plastered on every wall of the cancer ward. These ceilings were low, mottled by mold and peeling gray paint. The air reeked of sewage and death, and the wheels of the gurney rattled along uneven tiled floors.

I tried to speak, but I only added my moan to the horrible chorus.

One of the men went to retrieve a cloth from his pocket, but the other stopped him. "You don't have to now," he hissed. "No one can hear her down here."

Doors lined the hallway, some open, some shut. The moaning grew louder, mixed with the muffled sound of sobbing. They pushed me quickly, but I still saw gurneys and overflowing bedpans through the cracked doors and draped limbs with bedsore-ridden skin. I swore I saw a rat scuttle across the floors.

It occurred to me at that moment that I was already dead. That perhaps all my Sundays at church had not made up for my sins. I was in Hell.

"Oh, come now, ma'am," one of the men said. He must have noticed I was crying. "This is just another floor for the sicker patients. Doc doesn't like them upsetting all the people getting well. You'll be okay. You just need a little more care than most."

The gurney came to a halt, and I was wheeled into a new room. No windows. Dark green peeling paint. Again, the scent of death, as if someone had smeared it across the crumbling walls.

"Get some rest," he said. "A nurse will be here in the morning."

I knew he was lying through his gold-toothed smile. They'd brought me here to die.

The door slammed shut, and I was immersed in total darkness. I heard a man praying in the room next to mine in between sobs.

I wished I had my radio.

CHAPTER ONE

Matthew, 1992

November 13, 1992

I once was told the definition of insanity is doing the same thing repeatedly and expecting different results. I understand this because I do it every day. Load the typewriter with a fresh sheet of paper, expecting the words to come. But they never do. I'm worried they might not let me keep my typewriter unless I'm actively typing, so I've decided to create a journal. I can't say it will be very amusing, as I haven't kept a diary since I was a child, but I can say it beats my nightly pacing.

Despite whatever they'd given him for sleep, the sudden rap at the door made Matthew jump. Heart hammering in his ears, he smashed his cigarette into the nearby ashtray. "Hold on, please." He ripped the sheet of paper out of his typewriter and laid it face down on the desk.

The opened door revealed a dishwater blonde with smudged eyeliner. "You got a smoke?"

Matthew frowned.

The young woman standing before him was painfully thin, wearing nothing but a beige slip dress that clung to her protruding bones. Her hair was a mess of tangles, struggling to be contained in a braid draped down her chest.

Matthew scanned the shadowy hallway behind her. "Are we allowed to be up and about this late?"

She snorted and pushed her way into the room. "We can do whatever we want. This isn't a hospital."

"That's what everyone keeps telling me," Matthew sighed, shutting the door behind them.

She quickly located his half-smoked pack of cigarettes on the table next to a book of matches. Then she flopped down on the plastic-covered couch and lit one, studying Matthew's face while she inhaled. "Groovy glasses," she offered.

"Um, thank you. I'm blind as a bat."

She didn't respond, her eyes continuing to scan the room.

Matthew suddenly felt self-conscious. He'd done nothing since his arrival; the pathetic bag he'd thrown together in a frenzy still sat unpacked in the corner. At least his bed was still made.

"So, what are you here for?"

"I can't sleep," he quickly replied, pushing away the vision of Robert's heartbroken face before it surfaced.

The woman squinted, accentuating the premature wrinkle lines on her face. "There's got to be more to it than that."

"Why are *you* here?"

"I'm a druggie," she said with a shrug. "My agent is tired of dealing with me. I just bombed an audition for All My Children, and if I don't get another gig soon, my career is over."

Matthew blinked when she recognized her. "You're Cindy Warren."

She took another hit. "And you're Matthew Collins. The New York Times Bestselling Author."

Matthew felt the blood drain from his face.

"Take a chill pill. You look nothing like you used to. I doubt anyone here reads sci-fi, anyway."

Matthew did not respond. People finally stopped recognizing him a few years back, around the time he and his agent parted ways.

How ironic to be reminded of his washed-up writing career so far from New York City, where he lived and wrote for years. Before he got sick and went into isolation.

"I can't sleep either, so I sneak around," Cindy continued. "The security guards play poker in the basement every evening at two, giving me free rein. I got into the intake office last night." She smiled mischievously. "I read your file."

"I have a file?"

"We all do. It just says the basics until you meet Doc, the owner of Meadowbrook. Then he'll take all sorts of notes. He's kind of a fruitcake."

"Doc? I thought this wasn't a hospital."

Cindy brightened. "Oh hey, do you wanna sneak into the office with me? It's almost two now. Maybe we can find something interesting."

Matthew glanced back at his typewriter.

"Come on," she said with pleading brown eyes. "What else are you gonna do tonight? Write on that thing?"

The halls were eerily quiet, and though Matthew told himself it was because of the late hour, he couldn't help but feel unsettled. It felt odd to be in a collective space with no murdering voices or muted television hum. There were no overhead lights either, only dim yellow wall sconces lining the halls. Every room they passed was dark.

Was no one else here?

Matthew barely remembered the night of his arrival when a stockinged woman with badly blended rouge—who made it very clear that she was *not* a nurse—took him to his room. He spent the entire evening reading until the woman came back with breakfast, then again with dinner in the afternoon. That time, she came with a small pill.

"It's an herbal supplement for sleep," she explained. "You're going to need your rest. Tomorrow is a busy day."

"Do you know why I'm here?" he asked her.

Her face had been impassive. "I'm not privy to personal information. I only know that you booked yourself a room with no check-out date. I assume you'll be staying for a while."

At that point, he nodded and wordlessly took the pill.

Cindy proved a superior tour guide, reciting everything she'd learned during her nightly explorations. Even hushed, her voice bounced along the painted beige walls in a soft echo. "This used to be a pretty rad hotel back in the day. There was a nearby concert arena that people from all over would drive in from, but when they moved it to the city, the hotel went under. Dr. Dobby bought it just in time. He likes me despite all my antics, so he told me all about it. I guess they were thinking about making it a hospital, but who would come all the way out here just for medical treatment? We're in the boonies."

"It looks older than that," Matthew remarked, recalling the towering edifice that greeted him after miles of rolling landscape. He'd had a brief thought to call Robert and tell him he was staying in a castle on a mountain, like the barons in Robert's beloved Gothic novels. Tears had threatened to surface when he realized he couldn't. He wouldn't. It was better this way—a clean break without any extra details. He refused to let Robert watch him die.

"Oh yeah, it was. This part is an addition to what used to be the servant's quarters, so it's kinda boring. I think the original building is from the 1800s," Cindy said. "Oh my God, did you see the old lobby?"

"I came through the side entrance and went straight to my room."

She grabbed Matthew's arm and pulled him down the hall. "You're going to absolutely lose it."

At the end of the hall stood a drab golden elevator, so old it still had a gate and indicator needle. Before Matthew could panic at being thrust into something that appeared barely functional, Cindy hurried him in and shut the gate with a slam. She hit the brassy button next to a faded L, and with a mechanical groan, they descended. Matthew gripped what he could until the car stopped with a violent thud, causing him to stumble from the impact.

"Cool, huh?" Cindy grinned as she helped him up. Matthew noticed she had veneers.

He meant to respond, but she pried open the door, and the view beyond seized his attention.

It was as if they'd been transported through time. The lobby shimmered gold, from the arches that topped each ornate column to the ostentatious chandeliers hanging from the high ceilings. Ceramic sculptures decorated every wall sconce and topped the posts on the staircase. Faded burgundy carpet lined pristine marble floors.

Discovering something so deliciously historical tugged at Matthew's creative mind. This place breathed untold stories. He located the massive concierge desk, running his fingers over the smooth mahogany as he imagined dozens of gold room keys where spiderwebs now dangled.

Cindy slid behind the desk. "Welcome to Meadowbrook, sir," she said in an exaggerated, pompous voice. "Will you be checking in?"

"We should explore the rooms," Matthew suggested excitedly.

Cindy disappeared below the desk. After a brief sound of rummaging, she popped back up, triumphantly holding a ring of old, faded keys.

Matthew grinned, though he wondered why no one had appeared yet to stop them. Surely, they didn't want just anyone exploring this part of the hotel. Someone cared enough to maintain its original fixtures; though aged, even the replacement furniture had been kept true to style.

"Come on," Cindy called halfway up the stairs.

Matthew followed, distracted by the polished wood carvings lining the stairs. *They sure don't make buildings like this anymore,* he thought, gliding his fingers along the grooves.

By the time he reached the top of the stairs, Cindy had already disappeared down the hall. Matthew admired the east wing's common room, its gaudy chandelier hanging above the circular red velvet sofa planted in the center of the room. The marble was cold and smooth under his feet. He could almost hear the constant ding of elevators, keeping time amongst the bustle of travelers hurrying to leave in time to make the train. He closed his eyes to picture flappers with short heels and bobs and smartly dressed gentlemen in suits. The Roaring Twenties, before everything fell into despair.

There is a story here...

"Hey, where did you go?" he called.

Cindy didn't respond, so he headed down the corridor, admiring the long stretch of crimson doors and squat, gilded vases at each separating wall. One of the doors had been left open a crack, and Matthew slid into the room. It appeared that whoever had renovated this part of the hotel had also maintained the lodging, for the room kept up the glamorous art deco style at a smaller scale. The same red carpet spread to each wainscoted wall, and bright floral arrangements topped every table.

"Maybe you should tell your doctor friend we need a room upgrade," Matthew half-joked. "I'd much rather spend my last days here."

Cindy didn't reply.

Randomly, Matthew thought of a dark pond he once found as a kid. Alone in the middle of the woods with no one around him, he couldn't help but imagine all the unseen, revolting creatures that lurked at the bottom, preparing to slither out from the mire and drag him back down with them. He'd raced back to the campground filled with such terror that he hated dark water ever since. Before he left, he told Robert that that was what being terminally ill felt like—slowly drowning in murky water.

"Hey, we should probably get back," he told Cindy, suddenly unnerved.

She had sprawled herself along the queen-sized bed, and as Matthew moved toward her, he noticed bruises along her pale, exposed limbs.

"I don't blame you for wanting to stay—" His words caught.

Shock took over, letting him know he didn't have to worry

about why the woman he'd just spoken to a few minutes ago was in an advanced state of decay on the bed. Or why the skin of her face had already begun to peel back to reveal a skull with no teeth. Or why cadaveric spasm had tightened her grip around the type of needle that hadn't been used since the earlier part of the century.

His shock let him know he didn't need to solve those puzzles, he just needed to flee as fast as he could. He bolted from the room, trying to hold back a frantic, burgeoning scream as he rounded the corner so fast that his socks slid on the marble. He tried to catch his balance, but the speed of his mad dash told him it was too late.

He didn't get to admire the railing as he went tumbling down the stairs.

CHAPTER TWO

Olivia, 1985

That night, she dreamt of a woman trapped in yellowing wallpaper.

Telling herself she wasn't crazy had become her regular mantra, and when she violently woke and dove at the wall to free the trapped woman, she whispered it to herself as Josh shook his head.

"Liv, we gotta get you some help," he sighed.

I'm not crazy. I'm not crazy.

She repeated it that afternoon as she sat in her office staring at her blank typewriter when she heard his voice echoing down the hall. She didn't strain to hear—she knew exactly what he was doing.

She combed her hair with her fingers. She couldn't remember the last time she showered. The last time she hadn't worn a ratty old bathrobe as she shuffled from kitchen to office to bathroom. She imagined her closet full of designer skirts and silk blouses retaining a layer of dust. The bottles of nail polish and high heels abandoned. Ruined hairspray. Molding make-up.

"Does makeup grow mold?" she asked Josh as he appeared in the doorway.

"Your dad and I have been talking."

Olivia sighed, her gaze drifting toward the open window. A

woman in the apartment building across from them watered dying plants. "You're sending me away?"

He shifted uncomfortably. "No, no. We booked you a stay, like at a hotel. They keep things totally private, so you don't have to worry about the paper finding out. Celebrities go there when they need a break."

"I'm not a celebrity."

"You used to be," he muttered.

Sometimes, when she looked at him, she could still see the young man she fell in love with a decade ago. He'd kept the same level of emotional maturity, but the outer husk had aged. Refusing to give up, he still wore the open shirts and bell-bottom jeans that were popular in high school. Lately, he'd begun brushing his curls forward to hide his receding hairline. Wearing cologne. When he started going to the gym for the first time after three years, she knew what he was up to. And now, it was time to get rid of the dead weight. He'd found something new.

"You used to be so beautiful," he said, pretending to be endearing. "Now you barely even brush your hair. The paper will never take you back like this, and your leave is almost up. It's been months since the accident. You need help."

"What time will the taxi be here?"

He sighed. It was the sigh of a man who could no longer control his perfectly manufactured life. His perfect, accomplished journalist fiancée. "He's coming now," he replied. "I already packed your bags."

Olivia ripped open a drawer and fished out an old pack of cigarettes, ignoring his look of disgust as he walked away. She'd picked them back up after years, and the very thought of it drove him mad.

The taxi arrived within ten minutes, unheard of in New York City. Josh must have paid him extra to hurry. She wondered if he'd wait until she was there to call his new toy or if he'd pick up the phone the moment she climbed into the cab.

He scooped in breath and held his nose as he gave her an

obligatory hug goodbye, lest his precious olfactory senses be offended by her daily perfume of cigarette smoke and body odor. Then he was gone, slamming the door behind him.

He didn't even wave goodbye.

"So, you're headed to the country?" the cabby casually asked as he screeched away from their apartment building and into the chaos of late morning traffic.

"Can I smoke in here?"

"Just roll down the window, please."

The soft-spoken Italian man must have realized she didn't want to talk because, eventually, the speakers hummed low radio music.

Olivia watched out the window as the blocks of cityscape gradually devolved into rows of maples and oaks still clinging to their autumn leaves. *Was it October? November?* Regardless, the sight of trees uplifted her, reminding her she wouldn't have to talk to or look at Josh for days.

She imagined him and her absent, arrogant father pretending to care about the state of her well-being as they planned her excursion. It made her think of a list she once found as part of a historical research paper in college. It came from a psychiatric institute, and it listed all the acceptable reasons to institutionalize your wife, citing reasons such as disagreeableness, laziness, or reading a novel.

Jerry: "Yes, she has dissolute habits and is prone to laziness, sir. We must put her away."

Father Figure: "I agree. I have no doubt she is as terrible a wife as she was a daughter."

"Is something funny?" the cabby asked.

She realized she'd laughed out loud. "Sorry, I'm certifiably crazy," she explained. "Are we almost there?"

"We have one more hour to go," he said nervously. "Do you need a rest stop?"

"I'm fine," she assured him.

Olivia returned her gaze out the window, noticing the city smog had fully dissipated. They were officially in the countryside.

The cab driver took the next exit off the highway and onto a country road, something that normally terrified her. Fortunately for all involved, she no longer cared about anything. After a good twenty minutes of watching farmland roll by, interrupted by a dilapidated town or two, her eyes grew heavy. She must have slipped off, for only moments later, the breaks creaked the cab to a halt.

Her eyes popped open, struggling to adjust to the light. A stiff woman in formal nursing attire waited on the massive front steps of a towering building, a tall African-American man in street clothes beside her.

The cab driver offered them a quick wave from the car, then moved to gather her bags out of his trunk. Olivia pulled herself out of her seat, squinting as the late afternoon sunlight put her eyes through another round of torture. The hotel seemed to stretch endlessly into the sky.

"You must be Olivia," the woman said warmly, though her expression was far from it. Disapproving eyes swept over Olivia's unkempt hair and house shoes.

"Call me Liv."

"I'm Mrs. Bartleby, and this is Percy, my assistant. We call him Junior." She gestured to the quiet man standing next to her.

Olivia searched, but she couldn't read the dark eyes settled below his heavy brow. They seemed vacant as if the body was fully present but left the mind someplace else.

"We're here to help you to your room," Mrs. Bartleby explained.

Junior towered over the cab driver as he handed off her bags.

"I was instructed to—" the cabby began.

"Thank you, we'll take it from here," Mrs. Bartleby interrupted, offering him a tight smile.

The cab driver looked grateful to take his leave of Olivia and gave her a quick nod before jumping into his car. Then he sped off in a cloud of dust. She noticed the entire parking lot was unpaved, the winding driveway lined with unkempt bushes and trees.

"Right this way," Mrs. Bartleby said sharply, pulling Olivia's focus back to her.

The sun successfully obscured her vision of the hotel, but it seemed oddly large for some simple countryside retreat. This was further confirmed by the interior; it was as though someone had put the entire building into a time capsule, let it sit for fifty years, and then took it out to polish it up for one last chance to shine. An oversized stone fireplace blazed in the center of the room, and Olivia's slippers slid across antique marble that still sparkled under the vintage chandeliers. Her guides wove her quickly through re-upholstered furniture, past a colossal front desk left no longer in use. The grandiosity subsided as they entered the east wing of the building, and Mrs. Bartleby paused at a modern elevator, misplaced amongst all the vintage 1920s decor.

Olivia hesitated. There was always the fear of getting trapped in one, and she certainly didn't want to be trapped in one with an angry-looking nurse and a tall, silent man with empty eyes.

Mrs. Bartleby hit the button for the fourth floor, provoking Olivia to step forward before the doors closed. She swallowed as the elevator lurched, praying to a God she didn't believe in that there wouldn't be some wild manufacturing malfunction. Besides the creak and moan of machinery, the elevator car was silent. The man called Junior stared off into the distance as though there wasn't a woman standing next to him wearing a fuzzy, moth-eaten bathrobe poorly hidden under last year's trench.

Gratitude washed over her when the elevator screeched to a halt and opened to reveal a wing that seemed much more modern than the main floor. Though its walls were beige and its furnishings spartan, remnants of what must have been a great fountain sat in the middle of its lobby. It was in desperate need of repair; only one of the four mermaid spouts had survived, the rest just open holes with fishtails. The lone mermaid stared at Olivia as they walked by; as they drew closer, Olivia noticed she was missing a jaw.

"Right this way." Mrs. Bartleby dipped down a hallway, and Olivia hurried to catch up. As they headed down the narrow corridor with burgundy doors, it occurred to her that for such a large hotel, it seemed painfully quiet. In fact, she hadn't seen anyone else since she arrived.

Mrs. Bartleby stopped at the last room to the left. She fished out a set of keys from her pocket and unlocked the door marked 413. Junior strode in before her, set Olivia's bags down, and walked right back out. Then Mrs. Bartleby entered, gesturing for Olivia to follow.

Sunlight burst through three tall, floor-to-ceiling windows, the wind tossing their curtains around the faded pink wallpaper that covered the living area of the suite. An old desk sat in front of one of the windows, next to a fireplace that dominated the nearest wall. A plain queen-sized bed covered in gaudy throw pillows leaned against the other one.

"There is a bathroom back there." Mrs. Bartleby pointed toward an adjoining room. "There you will find a bathtub and shower."

Olivia ignored her implication. "Thank you."

Mrs. Bartleby pulled out a brochure and slapped it on the desk. "Here is a list of all the scheduled activities and meals. Feel free to take time to get yourself settled. You are welcome to explore the east wing, but we ask that guests stay out of the main building. As you might have noticed, it's going through renovations." Her heels clicked along the wood floor as she approached the open windows to shut them with three loud bangs.

"Welcome to Meadowbrook."

Then she walked out, closing the door firmly behind her.

Olivia sighed and sank down on the bed.

The view was absolutely breathtaking from the windows; she must have slept through the part of the journey where they ascended a mountain top. She reopened the window, admiring how the sun dipped below the russet oranges and burnt yellows of the trees in the valley below.

A barren, unkempt courtyard lay below with what Olivia imagined was once a beautiful pool, swampy black water now stagnant in its basin. She shivered with disgust, quickly shifting her focus to the weathered gazebo and mossy fountains that ran as dry as the one indoors. *The writer in me would have once eaten this place up,* she thought. Overall, it was peaceful. Even more so because she was away from Josh.

She left the window to admire the rest of the room, running her fingers along the eighties-style wallpaper. "Should be yellow," she mumbled with a laugh. Her fingertips found a tear, and without thinking, she lifted the flap.

Like most refurbished places, there was a layer of older wallpaper underneath, though it was hard to discern the exact pattern. With a start, she realized it had been taped to cover up a hole.

No, she told herself, pulling away. *Journalist Olivia has no place here. This is a place to rest.*

She went to the bathroom and flipped on the light. The mirror reflected back a stranger, although she had Olivia's blue eyes and dark brown hair. She looked from the sink to the shower, observing they were both the dingy sort of beige common in hotels. She'd visited plenty during her time as a reporter, back when she could stomach the knowledge of murder/suicides and other horrid things that transpired behind closed doors.

Before the intrusive thoughts took hold, there was a knock at the door. She scowled, under the impression that her new friends would give her time to adjust. "Just a minute, please," she called.

The door had no peephole to prepare her for who was behind it, so she braced herself with a deep breath before opening it.

There was no one there.

"Hello?" she asked an empty hallway.

Her investigative inkling from earlier turned into a full itch. She'd entered a mystery, and the story had begun to write itself. She shut the door, wishing she had brought something to write on.

Her eyes again found the tear in the wallpaper. This time, she peeled off the tape, thrilled to discover the second layer of wallpaper did indeed cover a makeshift cubby hole in the wall. She didn't hesitate this time, pulling out pages upon pages of typewriter text. She squinted at the first page.

November 16, 1992

Things are not what they seem at this place. Whatever they have been giving me for sleep has been causing vivid, hallucinatory dreams. I believe they are to blame for my sleepwalking episode. I still have not been given any clear answers about the other night. My ankle sprain has been getting better, so I plan on exploring the grounds again tomorrow evening to discover my own answers. As of now, I have been told that the actress Cindy Warren does not exist. I don't know if I want that to be true or a lie.

"What exactly do you think you're doing?"

Olivia jumped as Mrs. Bartleby snatched the papers out of her hand.

"Excuse me, I was reading those!"

"What have you done to the wall?"

Olivia blinked, realizing she had ripped away an entire section of wallpaper.

"This is completely unacceptable," the woman fumed. "I will have to report this to Dr. Dobby immediately. I warned him not to put guests in the east wing, but he did not listen!"

Olivia tried to reach for the papers again, but Junior had appeared in the doorway.

"Junior, please fetch Lucy," Mrs. Bartleby ordered. "I'll need her to assist Ms. Olivia to the west wing."

"That is completely unnecessary—someone ripped at the wallpaper before I arrived." Olivia felt her blood pressure start to rise. "I'm not leaving this room."

Mrs. Bartleby's face had transformed into a twisted tomato as she turned, preparing to spew.

"I can stay in the room near hers, ma'am." A woman who could only be Lucy drifted into the room. "I'll listen for anything and let you know immediately."

"Thank you, Lucy. I will speak to Harold first thing tomorrow morning."

She marched out, clutching the typewriter pages tightly in her fist.

Lucy's waist-length blonde hair fluttered behind her as she moved to the bathroom. She emerged with wet hands from the sink, which she used to smooth down the loosened wallpaper. "There. All better," she said in a light, singsong voice.

"Who stayed here before me?" Olivia asked.

"I'm not sure, love." Lucy gave her a sweet, unassuming smile. The apples of cheeks radiated an artificial pink. "You can ask the doctor in the morning."

"I thought this place wasn't a hospital."

"It's not," she said sweetly as she headed out the door. "I will be sleeping in the room right next door. Knock on the wall if you need me."

———

"Can you tell me more about the hole in the wall?"

Olivia blinked.

The man sitting behind the desk was not a handsome man, but he wasn't terrible to look at either. Writers would have described him as slightly above ordinary. His eyes were a bland, grayish sort of blue that probably looked nice in the sunlight had they not been so buggy and obscured by wide-rim glasses. He wore sideburns that were in fashion last decade but kept the rest of his curly brown hair clipped short. His professional attire was outdated, but he wore expensive penny loafers, his whole look giving the impression that he wasn't sure what decade he was in. He and Josh would have been fast friends.

"Are you a shrink?"

"I'm a doctor," he replied with a smile. "I'm also the owner of Meadowbrook. You can call me Harold." He leaned back in his chair. "This place was abandoned before I bought it. I'm sure you can guess it was once a grand hotel. I'm a big lover of history, which is why I'm renovating it rather than tearing it down."

"I see."

"I wanted to create a getaway from life. Whether it's from drinking too much or the stresses of work, people can come here to Meadowbrook to relax. To heal from whatever might ail them." He leaned forward, staring at her over the dark rims of his glasses. "I do want you to relax, Ms. Caldwell. But I need to know why you're tearing up my walls."

Olivia sighed. "I told the nurse—"

"First, she's not a nurse. She's a caregiver here. Secondly, she said there were no pages to be found."

Olivia let out an incredulous snort. "That's because she took them from me!"

Harold leaned all the way forward in his chair, studying her face over steepled hands. "Your husb—"

"He's not my husband," Olivia blurted out with more venom than she had intended. "We just—we used to live together."

His eyes widened ever so slightly before his lips turned up into a smile. "Forgive me, *Miss* Caldwell. Your *inamorato* told us on the phone that you'd been dreaming of women in the wallpaper, like that old Gothic short story. Charlotte Perkins, was it?"

Olivia froze, immediately understanding his implication. Then came the chilling thought: *Did she just imagine the pages in the wall? Had it all been a dream?*

"The overly stressed mind often makes things more difficult for us, even creating things that aren't there. It's perfectly acceptable to display the behaviors that brought you here, but the fact that you're suffering from them so soon upon arrival lets me know you need to begin your treatment immediately."

Olivia began to protest.

"Your paramour also requested you have privacy, considering your career. It's far more populated in our west wing, so, as a courtesy, we put you in the east. But you have to understand, it's our most fully renovated wing, and we can't have guests just destroying our walls…"

"I—" Olivia realized it was pointless to argue. "Whatever you say."

Harold grinned. "Excellent. I'd love to show you something. Would you like to join me on a walk, Olivia? May I call you Olivia?"

The doctor stood, and she tried to hide her surprise at his stature. Olivia wasn't a particularly tall woman, but Harold barely reached her shoulder. *He is painfully unremarkable,* she determined. *Lost in the space between attractiveness and unattractiveness.*

"Follow me," he said cheerfully, grabbing a set of keys from his desk.

Olivia shuffled along, trying not to be annoyed by his pace or his upbeat whistle. He reached the elevator and waited with tapping feet for her to join him. As soon as she slipped inside, he bypassed the buttons with one of his keys. With a turn, the elevator jumped.

"What do you know about the Roman baths?"

"Quite a bit, actually," she replied. "I studied history as an undergrad."

He looked surprised, the first break in his overly friendly exterior. "Amazing," he said. "So did I. Before I went to medical school, of course. I graduated top of my class."

Olivia gave him a weak smile before the elevator doors opened, and she was hit with a warm, wet wave of chlorinated humidity.

"Feast your eyes on this," he said with gusto.

Her eyes widened. Before them were several underground pools fashioned to look like ancient Roman baths. Steam swirled around ornate fountains as they spit fresh water into the rectangular tubs. The pool bulbs were the only source of light, bathing the room in an odd rippling green.

"We finished renovations on these last week," he explained. Over the sound of rushing water, the open space created cascading echoes with his voice. "This was part of the original 1880s blueprint, but they never followed through. One of the later owners used it for medicinal baths, and another covered them with planks for a bowling alley. As you can imagine, that one never took off. Bowling, of all things." He chuckled to himself.

He went to one of the pools and knelt, swirling his hand around to feel the temperature. "I wanted to bring back the medicinal baths."

"I see."

"You can be our first test subject. It would be great for your temperament." He stood, still brandishing what was becoming a ridiculous smile.

Olivia blanched. "Oh no, I'm not really a big fan of water..."

"Nonsense," he scoffed. "Water can be very therapeutic."

"Really, I've been kind of afraid of it since I was a kid..."

"You met Lucy this morning," he continued as if he hadn't heard her. "She's agreed to administer your treatment down here, once a day, until you're feeling better."

"Honestly, my head has really cleared, and I don't think—"

"Are we going to have a problem?"

Olivia's words dried up in her mouth. Any bit of cordiality had melted away as Harold stared at her over his glasses, hands gripping his hips. She wasn't sure if it was because of the dim basement, but his eyes looked entirely black, as if the pupils obscured the irises. Her stomach sank as she realized all this time, she'd been looking at his mask.

Thankfully, the elevator blinged, and the woman who had entered her room earlier appeared. In her arms were several towels. "Hello, there," she said with a smile.

Normally, she'd have no issue marching right up to the woman and ordering her to corroborate the truth about last night, but Olivia felt frozen in place. She was too shaken to do anything but offer a weak wave hello.

"Ah, Lucy, you're just in time." The doctor had composed himself, back to all smiles.

The young woman walked forward, the humidity causing a dewy glow beneath her ash-blonde hair. "Dr. Dobby says you're ready for your first treatment?" She looked at Olivia with gentle brown eyes.

Olivia found she could do nothing but nod.

"Excellent," the doctor said with a clap. "Olivia, I'll catch up with you later. I have other patients to attend to. You're in good hands with Lucy. She's been with me for years."

"I thought this wasn't a hospital," Olivia whispered as the elevator doors closed behind him.

"I'll need you to take everything off." Lucy thrust two folded towels into her arms. "There's a changing area right over there."

Olivia nodded and carefully maneuvered around the pools, trying not to slip on the slick floors. Her cheeks burned as she walked, playing her interaction with the doctor back in her mind. Something about him unnerved her in a way she couldn't quite pinpoint. She was also furious with herself for agreeing to something she did not want to do to protect her goddamn reputation.

The changing area looked like a typical spa bathroom, and she imagined it would feel quite cozy when filled with people. Now, it felt strange being alone in something so cavernous. She located several monogrammed robes hanging on the far wall near the toilet stalls, and she set the towels down on the counter to retrieve one. Then she went into one of the stalls out of habit and peeled off her t-shirt and jeans.

Olivia tried to correct her dismal thoughts—taking a dip would be just like taking a bath. Nothing to fear. She'd taken plenty of baths, even after she started developing an aversion to water. She closed her eyes, forcing the memories of the incident away. That stupid goddamn boat Josh had insisted they buy, the feeling of salt water being expelled from her lungs as she fought for her life on shore. She'd been able to push through quite a bit in her lifetime, but getting over near-drowning wasn't something that came easy.

Olivia hurried out of the changing room to see Lucy leaning over the edge of one of the pools, pouring a translucent, lilac-colored liquid into the water.

"What is that?" Olivia asked, startling her.

"You scared me," Lucy said with a nervous smile. She stood, corking the vial and sticking it back into her pocket. "It's an herbal solution," she explained. "The exact recipe has been used right here in this hotel since its conception, made from water from our natural springs."

"Natural springs?"

"Oh yes. Not far from this very building, in fact. Medicinal springs were all the rage back when the hotel was built," Lucy told her. "The nearby village swore it had magical healing properties, so in the 1880s, a man named Crocker built a railroad line right through it so the general public could access them. He then contracted a man by the name of Nathanial Issacs to build a hotel to accommodate the influx of visitors. The small town doubled within months, which they named Meadowbrook Springs."

"I had no idea," Olivia said, intrigued despite herself.

Lucy gestured to the steamy water, which now had a pleasant lavender scent. The aroma soothed Olivia's nerves, but she hesitated.

Lucy gave her an encouraging nod, extending her arm for support.

Olivia took a deep breath and let the robe fall from her body. Then she closed her eyes and stepped into the warmth of the pool. Lucy's arm guided her forward as she lowered herself onto one of the seats built into the side.

"In the beginning, the hotel was invite-only," Lucy continued. "It was quite an honor to stay here. People were drawn in by the promise of healing—some even said the water cured cancer."

"This place has quite the history," Olivia remarked, surprised to feel her body relax in the warmth. It had been so long since she enjoyed water. The more she focused on Lucy and her words, the less she focused on the prospect of drowning and of the worrisome dark pools at the far end of the room.

"Oh yes, very much so. It continued to be one of the most highly sought-after hotels, even after a tragic fire ruined the east wing." Lucy pulled up her pant legs and sat at the edge of the pool, dipping her legs into the warmth. "I hope you don't mind."

"Not at all. Is that where my room is?"

Lucy looked at her. "Yes. You specifically requested privacy, so we put you there. Most of our patients reside in the west wing. "

"Oh, right..." Olivia frowned. Harold had just told her that; how had she forgotten so quickly?

"After the fire, the hotel sat for a time," Lucy continued. "The lure of magical spring water lost its luster by then, and no one wanted to pay for the repairs. A couple eventually bought it, boarded up the ruined part of the building, and turned the operational parts into a boarding school for wayward girls."

"Wayward?"

"Women who had run-ins with the law, young girls who had become pregnant out of wedlock..." she trailed off.

"It's amazing to think how many stories are here," Olivia offered sleepily, fully lulled by the warm, fragrant water and the sound of Lucy's voice.

"Something you can write about, maybe."

For the first time in forever, Olivia didn't mind that someone else knew she was once a journalist.

"I can see why he chose you," Lucy said wistfully. "You look just like Lisette."

"I'm sorry?" Olivia tried to open her eyes to look back, but her eyelids had grown heavy.

"Even your body is beautiful."

Alarm fully set in, but Olivia found herself unable to stir.

"Just relax," Lucy cooed. "He loved me at one point, too. You'll have a wonderful time here once you get used to it all."

"Did you sedate me?" Olivia cried, trying to will her limbs into movement.

"You haven't slept in days, Olivia," Lucy said calmly, lifting her slender legs out of the tub. "It's only natural that you are feeling tired. You should close your eyes and let the water take you."

Olivia felt herself sliding out of consciousness, the soothing warmth of the water shifting into a thick, smothering blanket. She tried to keep her eyes open and her head above water, but she was sinking. It was the yacht incident all over again, but this was not her thrashing fight against the furious sea current. This was something far worse—a forced but gentle surrender.

"That's good, Olivia." Lucy's voice was now a disembodied whisper. "Let it take you."

From below the water, she heard a low hum, not unlike the Gregorian chants that once captured her imagination as a child. But she had no time to think. She was almost completely submerged.

The last thing she saw as she slipped below the surface was Harold Dobby joining Lucy to watch, their distorted figures hovering over her as she sunk deeper and deeper until her lungs burned as they had once before, and her world faded to black.

CHAPTER THREE

Cindy, 1975

Cindy stepped gingerly into the hall, pausing to shut the door behind her. It was so quiet, the gentle hum of surrounding light fixtures was audible. Today was the first day she hadn't been gripped by the agony of withdrawal. She still wasn't able to keep food down, but the cold sweats and cramps had dissipated. Being famished did little to help her walking ability, however, and as she began her limping journey down the hall, she wondered how long it would be before she collapsed.

She'd never bought into a woman's penchant for fainting, no matter how many times they'd written it into her scripts. She considered it a male writer's shortcut—*just make them swoon! Women always swoon.* She couldn't even count how many times she had to feign fainting during a scene. Sure, soap operas were intended to be dramatic, but if she had to fall into the arms of one more greasy set guy with wandering hands, she'd really lose it.

An elevator ding interrupted her thoughts.

She limped toward the opening doors, surprised to see a woman already inside. Upon closer inspection, she noticed the woman wore a smile so painfully wide that it obscured the lower half of her eyes.

"Um, hi," Cindy offered, assuming she was another patient.

The woman said nothing, her horrible smile stretching just a bit wider.

Cindy went to press the button for the ground floor but noticed that the buttons for every floor had already been pressed as if the woman had done it intentionally. The horrible look on the woman's face hinted she'd been at it for hours.

"Welcooooome to Meadowbrook. Are you suuuure you want to go to *that floor?*" the woman asked. Her voice was high-pitched like a child, distorted by her painfully over-stretched lips. "Some of these floors have ghooooosts."

"I'll just take the stairs." Cindy backed out of the elevator. "Enjoy your ride," she muttered as it dinged, encapsulating the woman back inside.

Vision wavering, Cindy located the stairwell at the far end of the hall. She hobbled down the carpet, not looking forward to having to use the stairs. She tried not to look down, the bright orange and brown geometric pattern taunting her recently quelled nausea. She focused instead on the walls, a gentle green that reminded her of a shirt she once wore to an awards show. Although she did get blood on it eventually. Her best highs were found at afterparties, entangled with some nobody in a sweaty room with dim lights, bottles of liquor, and lines of anything you could hope for. She suddenly thought of her track-marked arms beneath her sleeves and wondered how long this round of sobriety would take before they healed again.

Cindy had little hope of staying clean, but she did want to dry out enough that she wouldn't lose her job. While she longed to one day hit it big on the coveted silver screen, she made enough to afford a chic little apartment in Brooklyn Heights. Sure, it was currently trashed, but it was hers. She *owned* the damn thing. No jilted lover or estranged family member could take it from her.

She made it to the door under a bright, rude EXIT sign and pushed. The stairwell didn't offer much light, but she went forward regardless. It wasn't until the door slammed behind her did she realize it was actually pitch black. She searched her pockets for a lighter, cursing when she remembered they'd frisked her at intake. She'd have to feel her way down.

Come to think of it, the entire intake process had been a blur. Her agent had arranged a taxi, and she'd stumbled straight out of a party and into it, passing out immediately. She woke up in a pool of drool with her hair plastered to the side of her face. She faintly recalled the horrified look of the intake nurse, but the male orderlies were unfazed as they did all but carry her to her room. Without hesitation, she'd taken the hearty dose of methadone given to her and passed right back out.

It wasn't until Cindy's foot hit the second landing of the stairwell that it occurred to her that she had absolutely no idea where she was. She hadn't even asked her agent on the phone, nor did she look at any of her surroundings on the way in. The thought startled her so badly that she tripped on the next step and stumbled down the rest of the stairs until she hit the next landing with a thud.

Her groan echoed as she reached up to touch blood. "Fuck."

"That's a bad word for a lady to say."

She scrambled backward like a crab until she hit the wall. Blinking the blood out of her eye, she'd tried to understand what she was seeing. Holding an old-fashioned gaslamp, a little boy not more than ten stared at her from where he had been crouching on the floor. Shadows covered most of his face, but she could make out wide, blue eyes behind bottle cap glasses and curly brown hair. It wasn't his appearance that was terribly strange, but his outfit; he wore a pair of dusty, old-fashioned slacks and a linen shirt as if he'd walked right off the set of a historical TV show.

Confused, Cindy tried to stand but found her weakened state, plus the impact of her fall, had rendered her legs temporarily useless. "Who—where am I?"

"I was going to ask you the same thing," said the boy. "Do you know the year?"

"The year?" Cindy struggled to keep her head straight. "Look, I just got here a little bit ago, and I have no idea where I am or what's going on. I was trying to find the main office." She squinted at him. "Is that a gaslamp you're holding?"

"I'm not sure which door will lead me back," said the boy, rising to his feet. Even his shoes looked odd. "This is only the third time I traveled, so I'm not very good at it yet. Have you met Ms. Helen?"

"No, I haven't met anyone. I wanted to go to the office and ask for some food."

He lifted the lamp so he could see her, flooding the space where Cindy sat in muted gold light. It revealed three doors behind him, which confused her as she could have sworn she was in a narrow, four-floor hospital, but maybe she'd gotten the layout wrong. One of the doors looked strange, smaller than the rest, with a symbol etched into the paint. She thought of Alice in Wonderland. *Curiouser and curiouser...*

The boy wrinkled his nose at her outfit. "You're not wearing a uniform, so you're probably not trying to go where I am."

"Do you know which one leads to the main office?"

"No, miss, I don't," he replied with a disheartened sigh. Then he brightened. "Do you see the symbol right there?" He gestured to the strange-looking door. "If you ever get lost, just look for that symbol."

"Okay, thanks." Cindy attempted to climb back on her feet, managing to finally stand on wavering legs. She stumbled towards the closest door.

"Good luck."

She pushed into the door handle, and it popped open, causing her to stumble onto the ground. Tile, not carpet, met her knees and slammed into her chin. She watched tiny droplets of blood splatter onto the linoleum. *How many damn times was she going to fall today?*

"She's here!"

"Is that the missing patient?"

Cindy rolled over, squinting under fluorescent lights as two men loomed over her, one with arms too thick to be kind. Before she could speak, a young Black woman pushed past them, the tights under her nursing dress a blinding white.

"Yes, it's her," she said loudly to the crowd that gathered. She helped Cindy up to a seated position and examined her quickly, noticing the blood trickling down her forehead. "I'll escort her to the medical ward. She'll need stitches before she can receive her treatment."

"Treatment?" Cindy looked at the group of medical staff that had gathered around her. They were all badly dressed, as if someone had rifled through a thrift store to outfit the entire hospital.

"Don't worry about that now, honey," the nurse said in a low voice close to her ear. "Just walk as best you can, and I'll help you."

The thick-armed man scowled and crossed his intimidating appendages over his barrel chest. "Ya sure we shouldn't take her to the doc? Can't be having 'em running away like that."

The nurse met him square in the eye, and Cindy could almost feel the weight of her presence from where she sat on the floor.

"We can't take her to him bleeding," the nurse said firmly. "I'll bring her right back."

Miraculously, the orderly backed away.

The nurse helped Cindy to her feet. Then she let her lean into her as they made their way across the room. The crowd dissipated, though their eyes remained locked on Cindy. She assumed it was because they'd seen the show, but she couldn't understand why her agent would have booked her at a place where they'd make it so obvious. In fact, now that she remembered it, she thought he'd said something about how other stars went there for rehabilitation. *You'd think this place would practice a little discretion and tact.*

"When we get to my room, can I use the phone?" she asked the nurse.

"You don't have phone privileges yet, honey," she replied gently. "But you can ask the doctor after you're all stitched up. You were supposed to get your ECT treatment today, but you weren't in your room. You had the whole ward looking for you."

Cindy stopped in her tracks. "How can I already have a treatment plan if I just got here?"

The nurse's eyes swept over her face. Her kind demeanor

melted, making way for a somber expression. "You listen to me carefully—I am here to help you, but not everyone at this hospital is kind. You need to keep your voice down and follow my lead. Can you do that for me?"

Although Cindy's default reaction in these situations was defiance, something about the woman's eyes made her quietly acquiesce. That, and the growing sensation that something was very wrong.

The nurse guided her down a hall of open hospital rooms and lingering patients until they reached double doors with the words *Medical Ward* stenciled in black across the windows. Through the glass, Cindy could make out the frantic dance of white-cloaked doctors and nurses. She wondered if the boy she met had come from here.

"When I was in the stairwell, I saw a boy," she told the nurse. "Is he a patient here, too?"

The nurse stopped, her eyes wide. "A boy?" she repeated. "Was he a little Black boy? Where did you see him?"

"June? What are you doing?"

Cindy turned to see an older woman with steel eyes stomping their way. Her high-heeled shoes cracked against the linoleum floors, causing any dawdling patients to scurry away like rats. She wore a pinched expression, an ill-fitting cardigan cinching her heavily starched nursing whites. Her name tag read *Helen Bartleby, Head Nurse*.

The woman took one look at Cindy and gasped. "My goodness, what happened to her head?"

"She got lost and found herself in the stairwell," Nurse June explained. "Someone ought to talk with security about putting the lights back on in there. She tripped, so I'm taking her to the medical ward."

The older woman roughly pushed back Cindy's hair and huffed. "This needs nothing more than a band-aid. Think clearly, June. If she gets her treatment on time, Dr. Dobby won't know she disappeared for over an hour under your care."

"Now, Ms. Helen—"

"Wait," Cindy interrupted. "I didn't consent to any kind of treatment. I just arrived two days ago."

"Yes, dear, whatever you say," Ms. Helen said dismissively. Her fingers dug into Cindy's arm as she pulled her out of June's grasp.

Anger shot through Cindy, melting away any of her earlier confused trepidation. "Listen, you old hag. I'm getting tired of this shit. I want to speak to my agent right now!"

Ms. Helen said nothing, simply retrieving a thin whistle from underneath her cardigan. She put it to her thin, wrinkled lips and blew, summoning the two men from earlier who roared in. One brandished a needle.

Cindy panicked. "Wait—what are you doing?" She looked at June, and though her face did not move, her eyes swam with sadness and regret.

Before she could say anything more, the needle pierced Cindy's skin. In an instant, there was peace, all her withdrawal symptoms replaced by a flood of pleasure. She let the orderlies lift her up, feeling like an Egyptian queen being carried through the streets on a litter. They took her back down the hall to another set of doors. She didn't mind that the faces of all the people she passed melted from their skulls to create pink and red puddles on the tile. Nor did she mind when they put her on the bed and clamped down her wrists and ankles. She was flying higher than she had ever flown before. This was it—this was exactly what she needed. Who needed sobriety, auditions, diet plans, and creepy directors who talked her into late-night hotel meetings? The men who offered her whatever drug she wanted as long as she complied. This was so much simpler—she could just stay here in her warm, little bubble of pleasure without ever having to spread her legs for some sleaze with a comb-over.

But like all good highs, it demanded payment for its pleasure, and she soon realized a sacrifice still had to be made. But this was safer—more clinical—and she didn't flinch when the melting faces above her dripped on her lips, moistening them as they shoved a bite block in her mouth. She thought of the last director she fucked, of the yellow stains crusting the underarms of his white t-shirt as he told her to take off her clothes. She thought of the way he grunted on top of her like a greasy pig as they clamped a metal headband on her head.

She fell out then, before the first wave of electricity threatened to disturb her perfect high, the images of all the men fading into a black abyss, never to be thought of again.

The next morning, Cindy woke to the sensation of sunlight boring a hole in her brain. Her entire head throbbed, her thoughts muddled like she'd just woken up from a night of heavy drinking. She tried to piece together the events from the night before, but an empty, blank spot came up where her memories should have been.

She tentatively rose, noticing her clothes had been taken and replaced by a thin hospital gown. She shivered as the breeze from the nearby open window hit her skin, and she pulled up the green wool blanket around her shoulders.

"Good morning," a young woman said from over the pages of a faded magazine. Barely eighteen, she was reclined in the bed across from Cindy's, her feet twitching as she spoke.

Cindy realized they were in an old hospital room. "What—" Her graveled voice caught in her throat. Her mouth felt as if she'd been swallowing ash.

She tried again. "Where am I?"

The girl closed the magazine with a sigh. "You're lucky you're even awake at all. I've seen some gals come out of ECT like zombies. You only slept for two days." She crossed her legs and straightened her shift dress, its baby pink color clashing horribly with the room. The walls had been smothered with an ugly off-white, almost yellow paint and the bedspreads bore an orange and pea-green pattern that matched the shaggy rug on the floor. It looked as if they'd tried to make a hospital room look like a home, but the lack of lamps or tables, plus the bars on the window, made it very clear it definitely was not that.

The door opened suddenly to reveal a bespectacled woman in crisp, vintage nurse whites. It brought forward the memory of the Black nurse Cindy met earlier. *What was her name again? What had she told me?*

"Good afternoon, Cindy. It's good to see you awake."

"W-where am I?" she croaked.

"We moved you up to the medical wing," the nurse explained, handing her a few pills and a cup of water. "You didn't respond as expected to the last treatment, and we need to keep a closer eye on you. Lucky for you, Linda is a wonderful roommate."

Cindy looked down at the white and yellow pills in her palm. She recalled the glorious, dripping high from before. "What are these? Is this what you gave me before?"

"They're just vitamins to help restore brain function after your treatment. We can administer them intravenously like yesterday, but then I'll have to bring Dr. Dobby in here. You wouldn't want us to go through all that trouble now, do you?" She gave Cindy the fakest smile she'd ever seen.

Cindy swallowed the pills, following it up with a large gulp of water from the cup the nurse handed her. She was struck by how cold and crisp it was on the way down, soothing the heat in her mouth.

The nurse turned to the girl she called Linda to offer her the same pills. Cindy noticed two dark marks on the girl's temples as she took them without resistance.

"Make sure you're dressed for your walk around the grounds in twenty minutes," the nurse told Linda, gesturing to a set of plastic rain boots near the foot of her bed. Then she disappeared once more.

Once the nurse was gone, the girl turned back to Cindy. "My real roommate was named Beth." She tucked the magazine under her cushion and pulled on her boots. "She must have switched places with you."

"Listen," Cindy tried again. "I don't understand anything that's going on here. I feel like my brain got scrambled."

Linda approached her bedside. From up close, Cindy could see tiny little scars all over the skin on her arms.

"There are really strange things that happen in this hospital," Linda told her. "I don't have any answers, only what I can see. I am a patient here, too."

"Is...is this real?"

"That's a complicated question."

"Can you at least tell me where I am? I don't think I'm supposed to be here."

"We can talk after I get back. You probably should keep resting." Then, she left without transition.

Cindy felt a wave of nausea and fell back into her bed. The outside wind picked up the thin hospital curtains, revealing dozens of patients shuffling along the grounds without coats, even though the breeze was cool enough to signal the near arrival of fall. *Hadn't she arrived in the summer?*

She pressed her eyes shut, trying desperately to remember. It felt as though someone had come through and left gaping holes in her mind, filling them up with dense fog. She wandered through it, easily finding things like her name, the set of All My Children, her last glorious bender... *the boy!*

Cindy jolted back up, ignoring the pressure at her temples. The boy—she had seen a boy in the stairwell. *What had he told her? Something about symbols?* She shivered as her bare feet hit the floor. Determined to press on through any discomfort, she wrapped her hospital gown tighter around her thin frame and carefully walked forward.

Although most of the patients were outside, some still lingered in what Cindy assumed was the common room, babbling incoherently in one of the corners or sitting blankly at several whitewashed tables. Thoughts of her agent came floating back to her as she headed to what looked like the main nurse's office.

Sam had once tried to date her but quickly learned Cindy was not the type of woman men brought home to their mothers. Content with a few romantic trysts, he took on the role of her agent without a second thought. She trusted him, which had been stupid, because why did he never warn her about all the industry men she'd have to sleep with to keep her career? And why was she here, in a psychiatric ward, of all places? She paused, longing for the needled relief from before. Maybe if she threw another fit, the men with white coats would return with their drugs.

Ahead was a nurse's station with a sign that read: "Evaluation Center for Disturbed Women." Cindy made her way toward it to discover a nurse with red hair reading the newspaper as she sipped from a styrofoam cup. A staticky old television set blared incoherently in the background. Cindy squinted to read the headline of her paper: *JOHNSON ASKS 10% INCOME TAX SURCHARGE.*

Johnson? Confused, she shuffled closer, shocked to see the nurse was reading a copy of the New York Forum from 1967. Before she could wrap her mind around something so unusual, the nurse folded the paper. "Is there a reason you're not on the grounds with the others?"

"I-I just had a treatment, and they wanted me to rest," Cindy quickly explained. "I wanted to ask, when can I use the phone?"

The nurse frowned, deepening her jowls. "The doctor should have explained your treatment program."

Cindy tried to do her best to look endearing. She hadn't even seen herself in a mirror for days and hoped she didn't look too frightening. "I'm sorry, I don't remember what he said. My brain feels super foggy."

The nurse signed. "I'm supposed to be on my lunch break." She opened up a nearby file. "What is your name?"

"Cindy Warren."

She flipped through a few pages, her eyes resting on one for a few minutes before she said, "Ah, I see. And what did you say you needed the phone for?"

"I have to call my agent."

The nurse sighed again. "I can't let you use the phones without written permission from the doctor. Until I get a note, my hands are tied."

Cindy fumed but attempted to stay calm. "Can I at least see a calendar? I don't even know how long I've been here."

There was a loud noise on the television set behind them, and the nurse stood to shut it off. But not before Cindy heard the words, "As race riots continue to spread across the United States, American troops begin a new operation in the Que Son Valley. But protesters will not be deterred: the time to end the war in Vietnam is now..."

Cindy's body involuntarily surrendered to a shudder.

The nurse stared at her as she pointed to the calendar posted on the wall. "You don't look well. I'm going to have to phone Ms. Helen."

Cindy couldn't peel her eyes away from the date: August 4, 1967. The newspaper said it was 1967. The television said it was 1967. The calendar said it was 1967. That would explain the outfits, the decor, and the misplaced feeling of the entire hospital. Everything lined up perfectly...except for the fact that Cindy Warren had checked in to the hospital in May of 1976.

Cindy backed away from the desk as the nurse picked up the phone.

"Can you and Bill come up? Yeah, it's the delusional patient. Says her name is Cindy Warren, but I have her down as Beth..."

A million thoughts swirled through Cindy's mind, rendering her unable to focus on one clear, plausible explanation. This had to be some sick joke, maybe some kind of acting workshop her agent had set up for her. But why would he let her be injected with more drugs, let alone whatever they'd done to her brain?

Cindy felt her legs start to fail. This was all just too much. She longed to be somewhere else—home in her trashed apartment, even her cramped little bedroom at her mother's trailer—any place but here. Again, the vision of the little boy flashed in her mind.

What had he said? Dammit, Cindy, think!

She heard the sound of orderlies barreling down the hall just as she looked up to see the bright EXIT sign like a beacon of light. In an instant, she remembered: *find the symbol if you ever get lost.* She bolted for the stairwell, employing every ounce of energy she could muster. The cold metal handle hit her hands as she slammed into it, and she shoved the door as hard as she could. A warning siren screamed in the distance as they closed in on her, but she had already catapulted herself to freedom. This proved to be quite the mistake, however, for she wasn't able to stop herself from smacking so hard into the railing that she flipped right over it.

She manically thought of Alice falling down the rabbit hole as she let out a horrible shriek, flying past three flights of stairs on her rapid descent until she landed with a final sickening, teeth-shattering smack.

CHAPTER FOUR

Randall, 1969

Randall fidgeted in the orange plastic chair as he waited. Though a sizeable electric fan hummed loudly in the window, the air was too humid for it to do any good, and sweat dripped copiously down his back. He hoped it didn't show on his face; he didn't want to give his potential employer the wrong impression. He wanted them to think he was cool, calm, and collected. Not that he was any of those things, but he needed a job. Bad.

The door opened, and a lady in a pencil skirt and teased hair marched into the room, chomping down on her bubblegum with visible annoyance. She fell behind her desk and snatched a piece of paper to fan herself.

"It's hotter than Hades out there today," Randall tried.

She was not amused. "Can I help you?"

"Uh, yes, I had an appointment with Mr. Bennet. For a job interview."

She sighed, spinning in her seat to open the file cabinet behind her. She located a folder and slapped it on her desk. After a few moments of scanning the columns, she looked up with an arched eyebrow. "Randall Fitzgerald?"

"Yes, ma'am."

"Follow me." The secretary stood and opened the door behind her. Inside was one of the biggest offices he'd ever seen. "Go on in."

Randall awkwardly entered, surprised by the bold purple wall-paper patterns and brightly colored furniture all around him. It was like nothing he ever would have expected in a place like this.

"Have a seat, bud," a voice called from the adjoining bathroom. "Almost done."

Randall found another plastic chair to fall into as he heard the toilet flush. A rotund man with a red face emerged, tucking a stained t-shirt over his large stomach into the waistband of his jeans.

"Nice office you got here," Randall offered.

"Oh, this shit? Can't take no credit for it. This is the owner's. I use it on weekdays when he's away. He's a real flashy guy." Bennet grunted as he sat down, his overtaxed chair responding with a squeak. He searched his desk until he found a crumpled pack of cigarettes. He offered one to Randall and, after he obliged, lit both with a Zippo. He tossed it across his desk and leaned back in his chair to study Randall. "What kind of background you got in security?"

Randall cleared his throat. "Well, I worked at quite a few bars in my hometown in Kentucky, including a pretty classy joint called Bunny's. I always got the job done. Never had any complaints."

Bennet took a long, hard drag of his cigarette. "Look, Randall, I like to shoot from the hip. I ain't a fool. This here hotel is the type of place that attracts folks runnin' from something. Are you runnin' from something?"

He didn't give him a chance to reply. "Nah, I don't expect you to answer that. What I do expect is that none of your past follows you up here. I don't care if you're a junkie or you're trying to dodge that damn draft folks keep talking about—if there are any problems, you better see your way outta here fast. We are a fuzz-free zone, you got me? We keep you off the books—all pay is under the table. In return, no trouble. You dig?"

"Yes, sir."

"Now, this ain't no regular type of security job. We already have those guys—you'll see 'em in cheap suits. *You* gotta stay incognito no matter what. That means you gotta lie through your teeth to our guests. You can drink, smoke a little dope, gamble even, but keep it copacetic."

Randall thought back to the newspaper ad that brought him there. There hadn't been any description, just a phone number beneath the words, *Need Work?* He'd used his last dime to make the call at a gas station pay phone. After a bored voice answered to give him directions with no more information, Randall knew it wasn't going to be a typical job. His suspicions were confirmed the moment he saw the place. No one who built a seedy casino out of a fancy abandoned hotel in the mountains dealt in normality. "Yes, sir," he said.

"Good." Bennet smashed his cigarette into the ashtray. "Now I gotta tell ya, Randy, this place brings in some crazies. And I'm not just talking about when it was a psycho ward. That's why we need guys like you."

Randall nodded. "Not a problem, sir."

Bennet stuck out a fat, greasy hand. "Good. Welcome to Meadowbrook Springs Casino."

Randall couldn't help but grin as he shook it. Easiest job interview he ever had. "You won't regret hiring me, sir. I promise."

"Judy!" Bennet called. "Grab Randy here a key. And a map!"

"A map?"

Bennet chuckled. "It's a big hotel, Randy. Employees stay in a building off the west wing. We put our special guests in the east and the regular folks in the west."

"Special guests?"

"Everybody needs an escape. Even rich folks." Bennet shrugged. "Now, there are four floors, except in the east wing. Back when this place was a loony bin, some dipshit snuck over to the east wing and set it on fire. Apparently, he was screaming about how it was a portal to hell. Can't say I blame him; weird shit goes on here, but the only thing hellish around here is this damn heat wave."

Even in the warmth, Randall shivered.

"Anyway, when we rebuilt it, we added a penthouse suite on a new fifth floor. But it's private, so don't go concerning yourself with it. You can't miss the casino in the old ballroom, and we have a bowling alley in the basement—" He noticed Randall's nervous look and chuckled. "You'll get the hang of it."

Judy burst in, holding a bright blue key ring and a faded map. She handed both to Randall, wearing a face that looked like she'd just squished a bug.

Randall shook hands again with Bennet and headed outside to grab his bags out of the truck. The blazing sun had finally started to set, and he hoped it would take some of the heat with it. He noticed flashes of headlights in the distance as cars full of guests headed up for the night's amusements. For a place in the middle of nowhere, it sure did well, he thought. He jogged back up the stairs and into the lobby, where he unfolded the map. He found the path to his room, then shoved the map back into the back pocket of his Levis.

He headed through the lobby and past the old ballroom. He peeked in to see it still had remnants of its original gold fixtures, but with modern lights and signage. It echoed with laughter, the *chiiing* of slot machines, and the outbursts of gamblers standing around the roulette tables. The bar took up the entire back wall, and he noticed a few long-legged women sipping cocktails. It took him only a few moments to realize they were the high-class kind of call girls places like Bunny's could only dream of.

Soon enough. First, he needed to change his clothes.

It took less than ten minutes to navigate through the west wing to the employee building. The common room and the nearby kitchenette were surprisingly empty, but Randall figured everyone was busy; it didn't take a genius to understand evenings at a casino required all hands on deck. Beyond a string of empty offices was a hallway lined with doors. He found the one at the end marked 113 and turned his key in the lock.

It was a simple room but much nicer than any he'd stayed in the past few months. Cleaner, too. He threw his bags down on the bed and headed into the bathroom to take a much-needed shower. As the water ran down his body, washing away the grime of being on the run for months, he let out a deep sigh of relief. No one was ever gonna find him here.

It was almost eleven when he made his way back to the main building, and the casino was in full swing. He headed toward the bar and ordered a Skol, leaning back against it to take in the room.

Randall always loved casinos, even as a kid. His pop used to take him along back before they had the fancy gadgets they did now. Pops preferred poker and probably would have brought home good money from it if he wasn't such a sloppy drunk. On the nights Randall wasn't with him, he'd get himself blitzed enough to get beaten, robbed, and left for dead by the local train tracks. But his father's mistakes didn't stop Randall from loving the casinos themselves. The energy, the bright lights, the drinks, the laughter... It was intoxicating.

Randall shook away the craving and kicked back his beer. No gambling tonight. Maybe not ever. He was gonna work the job and earn enough cash to get himself far away from the loan sharks. Then that was it. It would be a low profile from here on out. He left the empty bottle along with some change and decided to explore the hotel a bit. After all, it was part of his job.

The main stairwell was made of dark mahogany wood and burnt-orange patterned carpet. The casino clamor grew softer as he climbed up it. It seemed the hotel had a lobby for each floor, which separated the east-wing rooms from the west, and he passed through each one on his way to the fourth floor. By the time he reached it, he'd grown fully winded. He paused for a moment to catch his breath.

Randall considered checking out the west wing first, as regular folks were usually prone to having issues, but he couldn't help the nagging urge to head east. He often regretted his curious nature, but he couldn't help it; he needed to know exactly what kind of rich people would visit a place like this.

Though it was far from the noise of the first floor, the fourth was eerily quiet. It was also strangely cool as if spared from the summer swelter, with its lights dimmed low. As Randall headed toward its lobby, he heard the elevator ding. He turned to observe an elevator so old it still had a gate. Above its gold door was a matching indicator needle.

Randall stood motionless as the door slid open, and a man dressed in an oddly formal uniform pried open the gates. He stepped out as if waiting for Randall to join him. "Going down?" he asked.

Randall stumbled over his words, confused. "I-I'm sorry. I didn't press the button."

"Ah," the operator said with a smile. "These old buttons tend to stick at times. When this car was first installed, it had a manual lever I had to hold to park it. I can't complain, though—it was much easier than the ones with pulleys. A man could work up one doozy of a sweat working one of those cars."

Again, Randall was confused. What the strangely dressed, chipper man before him said made no sense—there hadn't been elevators like that in operation for over fifty years. The heat was getting to him.

"Well, if you need me, I'll be working all night," the operator said cheerily, reentering the car. "Pleased to meet you, Mr...?"

"Randall. Randall Fitzgerald."

"Quite obliged. You can call me Jenkins." He shut the gate and waved before closing the door. "Welcome to Meadowbrook."

Randall wasn't sure why he felt so unsettled; why wouldn't some rich wing of an old-fashioned hotel have an elevator car operator? Rich folks loved weird stuff like that. Then he heard a strange trickling sound. Grateful to get away from the elevator and his thoughts, he headed toward the fourth-floor lobby. As soon as he rounded the corner, he was confronted with a fountain smack dab in the middle of the room.

It took him back for a moment before he chuckled. This was getting ridiculous. *Rich people really are something else.* He drew closer, and thirst lept in his throat. Crystal clear water poured from the basins of four beautiful mermaids into the wide pool below, enticing him. The fountain had been carved out of blue-green marble, and each lovely face beckoned him to drink. Beside the fountain was a table stacked with plastic cups. A sign nearby read, *Drink Me.* Randall, parched from the heat and the beer, happily obliged.

The water was so cool and crisp down his throat that he actually sighed with relief. He filled up his cup again and again, enjoying every last sip. Refreshed, he set the cup down and moved to continue his explorations.

The sound of trickling water followed him as he strolled down the main corridor. Each door was made of a dark wood that matched the railing of the main stairs, and the walls had been painted a shocking eggshell blue. It reminded him of the color of Lowcountry porch ceilings that his uncle used to call "haint blue." Although he was sure all the rooms were filled with guests, it was so quiet you could hear a pin drop. He figured they were all at the casino. Where he should be.

He started to turn back when two doors at the end of the hall caught his eye. The gold door numbers were all consecutive and odd until the end, where one was marked 419, and the other was labeled 502. He thought back to Bennet's words, including how the fifth floor was private, when a thought struck him. Poker games were almost never played out in the open; they were held in private rooms, far away from the other gamblers. That's probably what was happening in 502. Although Randall had told himself he wouldn't gamble—certainly not on his first night—there was no harm in checking things out. It was part of the job, after all.

He crept closer, the trickling of water soon replaced by an odd buzzing sound. He pushed his ear against it, when abruptly, the door swung open. Startled, Randall jumped back.

"Are you the next appointment?"

Randall tried not to look surprised at the heavily tattooed man standing before him. A joint was stuck in his ear. *This is who booked the penthouse suite?*

He thought about retreating when he remembered Bennet's instructions to be incognito, no matter what. "Oh, uh, yeah."

"Come on in." The man jogged back up the stairs that had led to the front door. "Hey, Lyle, your eleven-thirty is here," he called.

Randall nervously followed. He really didn't want to cause any trouble, but he'd been invited. Surely, it would have been more rude not to oblige. If things were shady, he could just make up some excuse and head back to the casino. No worries. He had this.

He reached the top of the stairs which opened into a flashy suite that reeked of marijuana. The suite was huge, with brand-new furnishings and bay windows that took up the entire back wall. Through fog from rolling tufts of cigarette and reefer smoke, he saw acres of rolling trees. But what really stole his attention was the shirtless woman. She straddled a high back chair, her breasts pushed into the leather as an equally shirtless, fully tattooed man dug into her back with a tattoo needle. She glanced at Randall as the artist readjusted, wiping the sweat from his brow.

"What, you never seen a gal get tattooed before?"

Randall stammered. "No, ma'am, I have not. Pardon my stare."

The woman laughed. "Aw, I haven't heard an accent like that for years. You're a Louisiana boy, aren't you?"

Randall stiffened. "Thereabouts."

"Relax. We all have something to hide here. Like me, getting a tattoo against my agent's—and parents'—wishes." She giggled, the joy her rebellion caused apparent.

"Have a seat," the man who had greeted him at the door instructed as he handed him a drink. "You smoke?"

Randall sank into the leather sofa, noticing the table before him strewn with hash. "I'm good with the drink."

"Not too much." The tattoo artist paused to warn him. He wore long mutton chops under a crop of unkempt hair. "It thins the blood."

It suddenly occurred to Randall that if he didn't come up with an excuse soon, he'd very well end up getting a tattoo. A sudden wave of lightheadedness struck him, and he nervously sipped his drink. He thought of the last time he'd been in a swanky hotel room...and the horrors that happened to him after.

The buzzing of the needle resumed, followed by the fresh scent of blood in the air. If the woman felt pain, she barely let on, sleepily examining Randall from her slouched position. "Have you ever gotten a tattoo before, Southern boy?"

Randall cleared his throat. "This would be my first."

"Man," the man across from him said with a laugh. "You're in for a real treat."

"I'll have to stick around afterward to watch," she decided out loud. "I love watching virgins squirm."

Randall blinked. He couldn't believe how much blood was being released from the tattoo needle, the syrupy red starting to drip down her porcelain skin and pooling on the floor. She still didn't seem to mind, instead staring dreamily out the window.

"Lyle loves tattooing women." The other man relit the joint that had been in his ear. "There's something so foxy about it."

The woman in the chair giggled. "Easy, Mark. He's not done yet."

Randall felt another wave of lightheadedness, followed by nausea. "Do all tattoos bleed so much?" he asked nervously. He looked at Mark and immediately wished he hadn't. Smoke drifted out of the man's mouth, his ears, his nose, even his eyes.

Randall had no time to react, for the second the man opened his mouth to reply, fire roared out. Randall jumped up in terror. Within seconds, the entire suite was aflame.

"Hey, pal, are you okay?" Mark asked. His face had started to melt from the intense heat, his skin barely hanging on by his eye sockets. His eyes rolled back and forth as he spoke.

"I'm not tattooing a tweaker, Mark," the tattoo artist said. "Get him out of here."

The noxious scent of burning flesh hit Randall like a baseball bat as the smoke found his lungs. He coughed, his mind racing to find a logical explanation. Then it dawned on him: someone had slipped him some acid.

"No, no, I'm fine. I just...need to use the bathroom, is all."

Unwilling to see anymore, Randall stumbled into the bathroom, managing to close the door behind him. He found the toilet and retched, feeling like he was being turned inside out. When he opened his eyes, intestines and eyeballs stared back at him from the bowl.

Randall stifled a cry and dove into the tub. There, he curled up in the fetal position and rocked himself back and forth. He'd never done acid before, but he'd heard plenty of stories. No matter what he saw, it would eventually go away. He just had to get through it. He squeezed his eyes shut and murmured to himself as he rocked. *It'll pass, it'll pass...*

His mind swirled with vivid pictures, like movie stills flitting across his eyes. He watched as C-123 planes zoomed through blood-red skies, spraying poison below. He saw fighter jets and bombs, and women and children being blown to pieces. He saw his father being beaten and heard the sickening smack of steel-toe cowboy boots hitting bone. When he couldn't take it anymore, he stood, prepared to flee the room. He threw back the tub curtain and saw a woman in a fancy dress. He thought she was a woman anyway, but he couldn't tell because her head was missing, flames creeping up the pink folds of her dress.

He screamed then, his feet slip-sliding in the tub until he fell, and his head cracked the edge with a loud smack.

It was pitch black when he regained consciousness, pain piercing angrily through his skull. His mind felt jumbled and thick, just like the feeling after a night of heavy drinking. He groaned as he sat up and nervously peered around the shower curtain. Everything seemed normal; he didn't even hear any voices or the tattoo gun. He winced at the thought of his hasty exit. He'd made a fool of himself, and now he was stuck in a hotel bathroom on a floor he wasn't supposed to be on. He had to get out of here before Bennet found out.

He climbed out of the tub slowly, squinting in the dark to find a light switch.

"Even if you find one, it won't work," a voice said.

Randall jumped back, his eyes frantically searching the shadows. "W-who's there?"

A man materialized in front of him, using a Zippo to illuminate his face. Behind a pair of glasses were hollowed eyes and heavy bags. He looked unwell, his cheekbones sunken in and his collarbones popping out of his button-down. Dark lesions had blossomed on various parts of his skin. "My name is Matthew. You're not supposed to be here. None of us are."

Randall dove for the door.

"I wouldn't do that if I were you—"

Randall didn't listen. He threw open the door and it immediately crumbled, revealing an ashy, charred room that looked as if it had withstood a fire but was ready to collapse at any moment. Its floor had caved in, creating an abysmal mouth with broken wood planks that jutted out like jagged teeth. He caught himself before he tumbled forward, and scrambled back against the bathtub. *God help me, I'm still tripping.*

"I tried to warn you," the sickly man on the toilet said. "You never know where you'll end up here."

Randall couldn't help himself; he burst into tears. "I never dropped acid before! When does it end?"

Surprised, the man seemed to take pity on him. He kneeled down where Randall cowered. "Look, I know this is hard to take," he said gently. "But we should probably keep moving. I don't know how we both got here, but if my calculations are correct—we're in the aftermath of the '63 fire. What year was it when you hopped?"

"Please," Randall blubbered. "I just want it to stop."

"Come on, buddy."

Matthew helped him to his feet and guided him to the far end of the bathroom. Randall realized it had the same burnt look as the rest of the suite, which was impossible if the man was telling the truth. There was no way he would have slept through a raging fire and come out unscathed. He was either still on the drugs, or he was dreaming. There was no other explanation.

Matthew searched the blackened wall with his fingers until he found a panel and moved it to the side.

Randall was shocked to see a corridor behind it.

"These passages were once used by servants in the early days of the hotel," Matthew explained. "They connect to all the rooms in the hotel. One of them has to have a solid floor we can walk across to get to the stairs. We can figure things out from there."

Randall paused at the opening, hesitant to enter.

"Trust me, we won't die," Matthew assured him with a hint of bitterness. "Harold won't let me."

"Wait. Please, just wait a second. So I'm not still tripping? This is real life?"

"Yes. Now follow me before the building collapses."

"I-I'm claustrophobic."

Matthew sighed. "Buddy, I'm trying to help you. But I'm going, whether you join me or not." With that, he entered the corridor.

Randall pushed himself to follow, more afraid to be left behind. But his heart rose into his throat the second he heard Matthew shut the door behind them. He led the way with his relit Zippo, but it did little against the darkness. With his arm, he swept away some of the thick cobwebs. Randall's shaggy hair took care of the rest.

Randall tried not to think of bugs crawling down his back. He tried not to let his claustrophobia take hold either, but every part of him wanted to flee the narrow, sweltering space. He didn't have another option. Logically, he knew the corridor had plenty of room to walk through—especially if it was intended for servants to pass through with trays—but he couldn't stop the feeling that the walls narrowed in on him with each step. He tried to breathe through it, following Matthew's hurried footsteps as he complained out loud.

"This is bullshit, you know. I had this whole thing mapped out, ya know? Cindy helped me. And Lisette, when she wasn't in one of her man-eating moods. I made my peace with death. I figured I'd just ride out the eighties. Wait for the disease to catch up with me.

But no. Harold can't stop fucking with the timeline. All I did was take the elevator one day. The elevator! And boom, I'm here. Oh, here, let's try this one."

Randall snapped to, observing the unfinished wood back of a door.

"Hold this."

The light from the Zippo trembled in Randall's hand, but he forced it still enough to offer a steady stream of light so Matthew could find a door handle. Hope flooded through Randall as he watched Matthew wiggle it a few times.

"It's stuck. Onto the next one."

Randall's stomach sank as Matthew took the lighter and headed on. Sweat poured down his back as he resumed his struggle to breathe. The corridor seemed to grow hotter and hotter the longer they walked, as if they were trapped in an oven. Randall tried not to let his traumatic memories push through, but he no longer had any strength to fight them. The last time he was in a hotel, he'd been invited up to play poker. The game had been fine—fun even—but just when he thought he had them all fooled, one of their bodyguards caught on. A day later, an old fisherman found him near the river, dehydrated and raving mad. *I'm not back in the trunk, I'm not back in the trunk...*

"Let's try this one."

Randall could barely stand let alone hold a lighter steady. But he tried his best, casting light on a strange symbol etched into the wood. He thought he should say a prayer, but no one had ever heard his pleas. Still, the symbol unsettled him, like something out of a horror movie, and he almost dropped the Zippo before Matthew gave the door a hearty push, and it creaked open.

Randall's eyes widened.

This room had not been burned at all, a lovely sun pouring through its windows. But that was the only thing about it that brought Randall any comfort. The room smelled of shit, piss, and other horrible things that made his eyes water. He saw at least a dozen soiled gurneys with people draped across them...what was left of them anyway. Emaciated and covered in bed sores, they alternated between soft moaning and the sound of weeping. It looked as if no one had checked in on them in days.

"What is this place?" he asked, horrified.

"Ah, we did hop again."

"W-what's wrong with them?"

"I don't know yet," Matthew replied. "Harold loves to run hospitals, and this looks like a sick room. Let's go. We'll figure it out later."

Randall noticed a cluster of flies near a window where a young girl had been stowed. She stared at him with saucer-big eyes, a thin string of drool leading from her mouth to a pool on her grimy pillow. He wanted to cry again, but all he could do was watch as one of the flies landed on her nose and walked all the way to the soft whites of her eyes. She didn't even bat it away. In fact, she didn't blink, the fly disappearing under her eyelid.

He fell back with a screech. "This is Hell! I'm in Hell!"

"Oh, fuck this already. I'm tired of begging you to save yourself." Matthew slammed the door, plunging Randall into darkness.

He screamed as he ran, spiderwebs filling his mouth and eyes as his throat continued to constrict. This was it—he had died in the tub, and now he was going to rot here for all eternity as punishment for his sins. He knew gambling was wrong—he knew stealing was wrong—hell, he even knew leaving that one loan shark for dead was wrong. All those years of running had finally caught up with him, and judgment day was here. He tripped and slammed to the ground.

Dazed, he began to sob. "God, forgive me! Please forgive me! Don't leave me down here, please!"

There was no response.

He continued to cry miserably in the dark until the thought struck him—Matthew had left him the Zippo. He pulled it out of the pocket of his jeans and flicked it to life, casting a weak glow on the lump he'd fallen over. It was a decomposing corpse, raggedy pieces of clothing still clinging to its bones. He could still see the

Levi's label on the waistband. Bennet's voice suddenly echoed in his ears: *"Back when this place was a loony bin, some dipshit snuck over to the east wing and set it on fire. Apparently, he was screaming about how it was a portal to hell..."*

Suddenly, everything became clear.

"Don't worry, Randy ol' boy," he told the corpse with a smile. The heat from the Zippo flame felt soothing in his hand. "I'm back to finish what you started."

CHAPTER FIVE

June, 1954

Shades of copper tarnished the clouds as the sun grazed the treeline. June usually loved watching the sunset, but now the sight of it filled her with dread. She nervously twisted the papers in her lap and watched the brassy trees pass by, their car stumbling along the dirt road.

Percy cleared his throat, his anxious tell. His hands gripped the steering wheel so tightly that veins protruded from his warm brown skin.

"I thought you said the hotel was up just a ways," she finally said.

Normally, when Percy spoke to her, he turned to meet her eyes, the side of his lip offering the slightest grin. He'd put his hand on her thigh, and she wouldn't be able to resist returning the smile. Now, he stared straight ahead. "It wasn't more than a month ago when I came up here with Dad. I know where I'm going." Despite his words, she heard the worry tightening his voice.

She looked down at the now twisted map and their copy of *The Negro Motorist Green Book*, knowing they were nowhere near any of the safe houses listed neatly in the pages. She could almost hear the disapproving click of her Auntie's tongue.

June had been raised wealthy in New York City, and though Mother and Father never spoke openly to her about the terrors of being Black in America, she needed only to listen to the world around her. It was her quick-witted, Southern-born nanny who formally taught young June what to fear. Auntie was the one who warned her about certain parts of New York, especially after the sun went down. "Not all cities like ours, June Bug. You always got to watch."

But Percy was her husband now. They weren't just childhood sweethearts anymore, they were grown and wed. A good wife trusted her husband, and June wanted to show him she did. Even when every part of her resisted the idea of a road trip to "break in the new auto" Percy's father gifted them after the wedding. Especially since it had been exactly three months since her last period.

They'd driven through miles of uninterrupted trees before finally reaching one of the country towns she'd been praying they'd avoid. Her skin immediately prickled with fear. Percy kept his eyes straight ahead, carefully maneuvering their Cadillac at a speed that wouldn't attract any unneeded attention. As if a shiny Cadillac itself wasn't attention grabbing as is.

The houses were in various stages of dilapidation, a few white folks minding their chores on their front porches, enjoying the September sunshine. June tried not to look in their direction, but she felt their eyes, and she knew at any moment someone could raise an alarm that would get both her and Percy killed. Despite her best efforts, her mind floated to the grisly images she'd seen in the papers. The photographs too horrific to see but too horrific not to print. She squeezed her eyes shut, trying to push them out.

"We passed it." Percy's voice cut through visions of lynch mobs and hanged children.

They were silent for a few minutes before June spoke again. "I don't think I want to go on another road trip, Percy."

"That really shook you up?"

June didn't reply. She opened the Green Book, distracting her mind by reading through the advertisements.

"There it is," Percy suddenly declared.

June's breath caught as she looked up. At the top of the mountain of orange oaks and yellow maples stood a four-story monstrosity. Flanked by two towers with steeple-like spires and large dormer windows, it cut a jagged profile into the sky. It looked like a building you'd find among city skyscrapers, completely out of place amongst the acres of untouched forest. She opened the crumpled map on her lap, scanning the landmarks. "Why isn't it on the map?"

"I told you, I came here before with Dad. When they built it years ago, they kept it a secret. Invite only. I think it was once a private hospital, too. This is the first time it's open to the public. I guess they haven't updated the maps yet." He looked at her out of the corner of his eye, visibly disappointed in her reaction. "Come on, ain't it beautiful?"

"Yeah. Beautiful," she echoed.

"I *knew* we were close. See, June Bug? Nothing to worry about." He grinned, and his hand moved to her thigh. But this time, she couldn't smile back.

After a few more miles uphill, the front gate appeared. It had been left open, the name *Meadowbrook* looming above them in fancy iron script.

"Are you sure this hotel is safe for us? It's not mentioned in the Green Book either."

Percy scoffed. "That book ain't all that great anyway. Dad wrote them for an advertising spot in the next edition, and they still haven't returned his letter. Can you imagine not knowing who Herbert Clark is? Disgraceful."

He accelerated, jolting them forward. Beyond the fading trees and yellow bushes that lined the long, narrow drive, the yard seemed well-maintained. In the distance, she could make out fountains and even the outline of a gazebo. Hunger bit at her stomach, and she put her hand on it, remembering her condition. Normally, the lunch they packed would have sustained her for a while, but her body was already changing. She closed her eyes. She'd have to tell him soon.

"Well, that's odd. There's not another automobile in sight."

June followed his line of vision to see there was indeed nothing but empty space surrounding the front of the hotel. Again, she was taken aback by the enormity of the building; for a hotel in the middle of nowhere, it spared nothing in its grandiosity. It reminded her of the St. Regis in New York City, with its windows that shimmered in the city lights, fancy architecture, and sculptured stone. But this hotel lacked the bustle; the only sound was the lonely September crickets belting out their last serenade before winter.

"There's no one here, Percy," June whispered.

He said nothing for a moment, just stared at the entrance. "There's nowhere else for us to go."

Abruptly, the front doors burst open.

From within the building appeared a white man with curly brown hair and a matching mustache. He wore no hat or coat, his suspenders holding up trousers that dragged in the dirt.

Percy motioned for June to stay seated as he carefully opened the car door.

"Good evening, sir," he called as he removed his hat. "My name is Percy Clark, and this is my wife, June. We've been traveling all day and were looking for a place to stay the night. My father is Herbert Clark, owner of Clark and Sons Woodwork. He put the new staircases in a few months back."

Miraculously, the man smiled. "Well, you two are in luck. I just purchased Meadowbrook, and we're planning a grand re-opening next week. We have almost everything ready for guests—you're welcome to come in and rest a spell."

Percy grinned, and his posture relaxed. "That's just about the best news I've heard all day, sir."

June did not exhale. She didn't like how the man looked one bit.

Percy moved to the passenger side of the car to help her out.

The short white man approached, the beads of sweat on his forehead catching the light of the setting sun. He extended his hand to Percy. "The name is Dobby. Harold Dobby."

"Great to meet you, Mr. Dobby."

"Unfortunately, it's only myself and a few maids, so I'll have to grab your bags," he said. "The cooks won't be in until tomorrow either, but the kitchen is stocked if you want me to fix you up something to eat." His eyes clamped on June as she nervously exited the car. They shone like beetles, boring into her as she took Percy's arm.

"You especially need to make sure you're eating well," he said. "Isn't that right, ma'am?"

Percy looked confused for a moment but kept up their friendly banter. "That won't be necessary, Mr. Dobby. We only packed one bag. And June here is a whiz in the kitchen. If you don't mind her getting in there, she can whip us all up a snack." He grabbed their suitcase before Dobby had a chance.

"Please, call me Harold," he insisted. "I'll show you to my favorite part of the hotel, and then we can argue about supper."

Percy went to follow, but June felt as if her legs were stuck in mud. Every part of her wanted to stay exactly where she was. There was no possible way that man could know about her condition—she wasn't even showing yet. She looked to the sky, the setting sun fully below the trees.

Harold Dobby gave her an oversized smile. "Don't be nervous, Mrs. Clark. All weary travelers are welcome here."

June swallowed and cast her eyes to the ground as she followed them up the front steps.

"Right this way," Harold sang.

June gasped as soon as they entered. Every angle dripped gold, from the dazzling chandeliers to the foiled ceilings that held them. Crimson rugs covered smooth marble floors, and fresh seasonal flowers created autumnal rainbows in golden vases.

"My word, Mr. Dobby." Percy whistled. "You really fixed her up something nice."

He beamed at the compliment. "Please, call me Harold," he said. "It was my intent to make her as magnificent as the grand hotels in the city, but with the gentle comforts of the countryside. I studied the original plans from 1886 and embellished them a little. I wanted her to shine like hotels did before the Depression."

"Well, you definitely succeeded," Percy said. He turned to June. "Isn't it grand, June?"

"Quite." June still couldn't shake her sinking feeling, even with the splendor that surrounded them. The hotel was deathly quiet, strange for an operation preparing to open. Where were the maids and hotel staff?

Harold ducked behind the great mahogany concierge desk. There were dozens of keys waiting in cubbies, and he selected the one marked 413. "I'll put you in the east wing, my favorite."

Harold beckoned for them to follow him down the hall until they reached an old elevator covered only by a folding gate. He moved it to the side, revealing a gilded car full of mirrors. He stepped aside for them to board.

June felt the room sway. She hated elevators.

Oblivious to her apprehension, Percy guided her in. Harold closed the gate, then gripped a long metal switch where the buttons should have been.

June's mouth went dry. "Where are the buttons you press for the floors?"

Percy chuckled.

Harold grinned. "This is the original elevator installed in 1889," he explained, "with a few tweaks to keep it safe, of course. You have to turn the lever and park it at your desired floor. Hopefully, I got the hang of it." Without allowing another word, he pushed the lever forward and the elevator dinged, then lurched. He watched June almost gleefully over the rim of his glasses as she pushed her body against the back mirrored wall.

"You're not looking so good, ma'am," he said. "You really ought to let me fix you all some dinner."

Percy took her hand. "Are you okay, Bug?"

She nodded, trying to stay firmly planted as the elevator reached its destination. "I'm just tired, is all," she assured him. She watched the floors pass them by, each with a higher, faded number, until Harold let the lever go, and the car came to a shuddering halt.

"I still got it," he said cheerfully. Then he opened the gate and the door that led to the floor.

June scrambled out as quickly as she could, not wanting to think about what would happen if the car started to fall as she stepped out of it.

Fortunately, the east wing lobby was enough to distract her. Though it did not have the same dazzling decor as its main foyer, it was gorgeous all the same. Instead of robust reds, the halls wore shades of blue, with an indoor fountain in the center of the room. Harold waltzed up to one of its marble mermaid spouts and took a loud slurp. He turned to June with a grin, wiping the water off his lips. "It's a drinking fountain," he proclaimed proudly. He gestured for her to follow suit. "Please, I insist. You still look quite pale."

June tried to decline politely, but Percy gave her a nudge.

She hesitantly bent, the ethereal mermaid sculptures eyeing her as she positioned her lips to a spout. She squeezed her eyes shut as she drank, thankful to taste cool, clear water. Instantly refreshed, she almost let loose a smile.

Harold grinned at her. "The water here is the best you'll ever drink."

Renewed by the slightest bit of relief, June followed the men as Harold took them down a door-lined corridor. She imagined what the rooms looked like behind them, pristine and waiting to be filled with travelers. Wealthy men wearing suits and plastered smiles on their pale faces. Snooty white women with red lips and oily rouge.

He stopped at Room 413 and pushed the key into the lock. The door opened to reveal a room with three large windows in the back, the curtains as blue as the sheets that draped the queen-sized bed.

"It's not the biggest room, but the view is spectacular."

"This is more than fine, Harold," Percy said, his eyes bright. "We can't thank you enough."

June's eyes surveyed the room, finally landing on the wallpaper of swirling blues. It looked brand new, displaying the intricate floral patterns that had recently come into fashion.

"Don't hesitate to ring if you need anything," Harold told them, pointing to the telephone. "Like I said, it's just me and a few of the maids here tonight, but we can help get you what you need. There will be a few guests here tomorrow—"

"Oh, we'll be long gone by then," Percy assured him.

June leaned in to examine the wallpaper, and though the room was warm, she shivered. The white roses looked like screaming faces.

She walked over to the window.

"Then I shall take my leave. Welcome to Meadowbrook." She heard the door shut softly behind her.

Right below their room was a swimming pool, the last bits of sunset reflecting off its placid surface. The crickets hummed as a cool breeze came through the window's open cracks. She felt Percy's arms around her.

"This place is really something," he murmured in her ear.

She whipped around in anger. "This place doesn't feel right, Percy. I told you I didn't want to stay here."

His face twisted into a scowl. "Only you would be unhappy at a fancy place like this."

"Don't you listen to a damn word anyone tells you? These places aren't made for people like us!"

"We aren't like the others," Percy snapped. "Both our fathers own companies."

June felt tears sting her eyes. "It's not like that in the country, and you know it."

"You need to eat." He decided, grabbing his hat. "I'm gonna go take Harold up on his offer and get us some food."

"No, Percy, please don't go—"

"You just unpack and get yourself cleaned up. Maybe take a little nap."

"Percy, no—"

But he strode out, slamming the door behind him.

She wanted to run after him, but she didn't. Instead, she fell into the bed and stared at the door until her lip stopped quivering. Then she stood, straightening out her skirt as she went to unpack their bag. Ignoring the angry white faces on the walls, she neatly laid Percy's slacks in the drawer, right next to a copy of the Bible. Then she went to the bathroom and set out their toothbrushes. The mirror reflected back a face that looked calm, serene even, with painstakingly relaxed hair pulled straight into a bun. The sunset that filled the room reached all the way to the bathroom, where it pulled shades of amber from her warm brown eyes. They were impassive, like her lips, pulled into a gentle line below the pearl earrings that dotted her ears. *My mask*, she thought.

She filled a cup of water from the sink and took a sip. However unsettling this place was, Harold did not lie about the water. It was cool and crisp, nothing like the tap water in the city. The cup clattered to the tile when she heard the sound from outside.

It sounded like a splash, and when she raced to the window to see what poor animal had fallen into the pool, she froze in horror. The murky water thrashed as two little arms reached out for no one, joined occasionally by a bobbing head that gasped for air.

June bolted out of the room and tore down the hall. She wasn't sure exactly how to get outside, but instinct threw her around each bend. If she was correct, she'd seen a little boy with skin like hers, not more than eight years old.

Her relief was short-lived when she found one of the exits, for she knew she still had to dart across the grass and through the courtyard gate. Her skirt ripped as she picked up speed. It had been a decade since she participated in athletics, but she was grateful for the hours spent swimming laps every summer at Camp Dunroven. Her legs were still strong.

She watched the little hand disappear by the time she reached the bend, the water still by the time she got there. She dove in without hesitation, realizing after that she had dived into a pool filled with stagnant muck.

She fought revulsion as she thrashed her arms around, feeling for anything that might resemble a child. She pushed up to the surface to catch a breath, ignoring the stench and the slime across her face and hair, before diving back below the surface. She wanted to scream, to cry out for him, but she knew she couldn't give in to her fear. She had to stay focused. Her toes and hands scraped the bottom of the pool, and she knew when her adrenaline passed, she'd have wounds to heal. But she couldn't think of that now, she had to keep trying. She had to save him.

She swam back to the surface for one more gulp of air. She knew she was getting tired, but she'd swam long distances before. She could handle it. She dove back under once more, swimming across the length of the pool with outstretched arms until, at last, miraculously, she felt a mass.

She grabbed it, ecstatic when his little arms grabbed her back, wrapping themselves around her neck. She bolted to the surface, breaking through and gasping for air.

She heard nothing from the little boy, but he held on to her as she swam to the edge. "Hang on there, honey, we're almost there," she gasped.

Still, the boy did not respond.

It had grown dark since she began her rescue effort, but moonlight peaked through the clouds. It sent a sliver of light over his face, which suddenly gave her pause.

"Honey?"

June froze.

The child that held onto her neck was dead. Not just dead, dead for so long that the skin from his face was gone, the thing holding her just bones with patches of rotting muscle and slime.

She screamed then, and the last thought she had as something pulled her back under the black water was of Percy and how she didn't even get to tell him that he was going to be a daddy.

CHAPTER SIX

Tommy, 1951

Today would be the day he killed himself.

For years, he had wished for it, but over the last few months, the longing became a plan. He woke up one morning with the shakes, struggling to put his morning glass of gin to his lips, and picked up the telephone. The operator found him the perfect hotel, a secluded spot nestled in the mountains, about a three-hour drive. He grabbed a bag still packed from his last show and his favorite guitar, assuring his wife he was just off to play another one. One of those spur-of-the-moment gigs. She could call his manager for the details if she really wanted. The face of the woman who was clueless that her husband never really loved her did not register any alarm. May just nodded in that pleasant, docile way she always did, like when he promised her they would try for children again. One day.

He called a taxi (he told May he didn't want to bother his driver, Joe, on a Sunday), gave her a quick kiss on the cheek, and left without giving it another thought.

The taxi cab driver kept his cool when Tommy tucked his tall, thin frame into the backseat, but as soon as they pulled away from the Hawkins mansion, he gushed. "Man, I've been following you guys since you played the clubs!"

Eventually, the cabbie understood the conversation would be one-sided, shifting the topic to the hotel. "They never get visitors no more. In fact, I can't even remember the last time one of our taxis got a call for Meadowbrook. It used to be a hospital back in the day, but now the only people who go there are the ones that don't wanna be found." He turned to Tommy and gave him a lopsided smile. "I bet that's why you want to stay here. Being famous has got to be exhausting."

Tommy did not respond.

When they arrived, he didn't give the hotel much of a second glance other than to notice how monstrous it was, perched like a damn castle in the mountains. He gave the cabby his autograph and tipped him well enough that he would drive off satisfied, then hauled his suitcases up the front steps and across the stained carpet in the lobby. The front desk was hard to miss, as it took up half the room, and he could barely see over the stacks of pots and pans on it, collecting water from the leaking roof. He finally located an older, heavy-set woman with a tight bun who looked at him with bored appraisal. "Checking in?"

"Yes. The name is Hawkins. Tommy Hawkins."

If she recognized the name, she gave absolutely no sign. She sighed, throwing her glasses across the book she'd been reading, and shuffled to retrieve a room key. She tossed it to him through an opening in the maze of cookware and fell back into her seat with a grunt and a cloud of dust. Glasses back on and face covered by the magazine, she gave no indication that she'd say anything more.

Tommy looked down at the key: Room 218. He supposed he would have to find it on his own.

Making his way through the lobby, he passed a massive, crumbling fireplace in the center of the room. His eyes trailed over what was left of its fine details, the care employed in carving each design letting him know that, at one time, this place had been beautiful.

Something to behold, but now in desperate need of repair. Deteriorating, rotting from the inside. Just like him.

He located the elevator down the hall, a dull and faded gold.

"Elevator don't work." The woman's bored voice stopped him mid-stride. "Gotta take the stairs." She pointed to a set of ominous-looking stairs down the hall.

By the time he dragged his bags up a full flight that offered him glimpses of abandoned hallways and flickering light fixtures, he almost regretted his decision to stay there. But once he shoved open the door to his room and drank in the stunning valley below, he breathed a sigh of relief. It was the perfect place to die.

He dropped his bags on the bed and headed into the bathroom. The toilet was cracked, and the faucet leaked, but besides the ring around the tub, it seemed in decent shape. For a death bath, anyway. He tested the faucet to make sure it worked, and after a few spurts of dirty, rusted water, it cleared, filling up the long rectangular-shaped basin. He peeled off his shirt and went to pour himself a drink.

Returning with a bottle of booze and a bottle of pills in hand, he briefly wondered if he should call anyone just to let them know where he was. He decided against it, not wanting to raise any alarm. He stared at his reflection in the water as it settled, imagining the old lady from the front desk finding his bloated body days later. Would she have the same indifference as when he first arrived?

The warmth felt wonderful on his tired skin, and he couldn't help but sigh as he lowered himself in. He remembered when he was a child, the youngest of seven, and the rare occasions he'd actually get a hot bath. Bless his mother—she tried her hardest to keep things fair. But she was perpetually exhausted until the day the angels took her at fifty-two. He'd moved on from a few drinks a night to a bottle then.

He eyed the pills waiting for him on the edge of the tub. He took a big swig from his bottle—it was cheap wine, just the way he liked it. It reminded him of poverty when he could stroll around La Marqueta in East Harlem as a skinny kid with no name. He knew it was selfish; he should be grateful for all the money. But no one quite prepares you for it. Or for the fame. One day, you're living life, playing shows, and entertaining the kind of women your Mami hates, and then next, you have a record deal and a tour schedule. You have no control of your life anymore, at the mercy of deadlines, interviews, managers. You take pictures, you sign autographs. You drink yourself to the point of oblivion every night.

It wasn't just that. He just needed life to be over. He'd reached the apex of the mountain and knew there was nothing left to achieve. It was all downhill from here, and he wanted death on *his* terms, not waiting around for some disease to wreck his bones like his little sister or a train to crush him like his Papi. He didn't want to make children and love them just so they would suffer and die, regardless of anything he did. All of it was so pointless, the fame and the money—it meant nothing. They were all puppets in a meaningless existence, just to one day cease to exist.

He took one more swig of wine and grabbed the pills. A handful at a time, he chewed and swallowed them, fighting the urge to gag until they were gone. Then he polished off his wine and settled into the tub. His stomach lurched, but he tried not to focus on the cramps. Instead, he pictured Mami when she was young, singing to him before he went to sleep. The way she used to run her fingers through his hair. The crushed pills hit him hard, and he was fading, smiling as he imagined her scooping him up into the soft, blooming warmth of her bosom.

He woke up on the bathroom floor next to a reeking pile of regurgitated pills and May's best roast chicken.

He retched again at the smell, this time in the toilet bowl. His head spun, and he cursed Bobby, his assistant manager. He'd asked him for the real strong stuff a week ago and was assured he'd be taken care of. He must have realized what Tommy was trying to do.

He flushed the toilet and used the sink to pull himself to his feet. Ignoring the haggard vision the mirror threw back at him, reminding him of his unshaven, sunken cheeks and disastrous black hair, he stumbled out. He'd just have to try again tonight. Maybe he'd use a rope this time or throw himself out the window. The acres of woodland below him would make for a beautiful last sight.

He re-entered the bedroom and immediately jumped back in surprise.

Knees threatening to buckle, he steadied himself against the wall. "What the hell..."

His room had been in decent shape on arrival, but it was nowhere near as pristine as the vision now before him. Fresh paint and elaborate wainscoting covered the walls between sparkling windows, and lush, rose-patterned fabrics draped the bed and pillows. A small chandelier hung from the ceiling that matched the gold bedside lamp, and a patterned rug lay at his feet. For a moment, he thought he might have wandered into another hotel room, but his guitar and his suitcase sat on the bed, just where he had left them.

Tommy took a moment to catch his breath. Maybe he had just assumed the hotel room was as rundown as the rest of it—maybe they kept their rooms clean for their customers. He wiped his mouth to clear any remnants of vomit as he stumbled for the door.

His theory was wrong.

The hallway, too, had been restored. A pattern of intricate wall sconces and polished doors led the way to a fully operational elevator that opened to reveal a well-dressed couple who laughed as they made their way to their room.

"Excuse me, sir," a man said pleasantly as he passed Tommy, tipping the type of hat he remembered street guys wearing when he was a boy.

He hurried to shut the door before anyone noticed his frantic state. His entire world was spinning, the impossibility of his situation worsening his already befuddled state. He took a moment to collect himself when the answer came to him: booze.

He tore apart his suitcase, finding one of his flasks that had, mercifully, not been drained. He took it all down in one gulp, letting the heat soothe his nerves and clear his mind. Then he flew to the bathroom to splash cold water on his face. If he was going to figure out what the hell was going on, he needed more to drink. To get more to drink, he'd need to talk to people. To talk to people, he needed to look like a human.

Grateful he had fresh clothes in his suitcase, he hurried to dress himself and ran a comb through his hair. Miraculously, his pomade hadn't washed off in the tub, keeping his stubborn locks at bay. He shook his head, realizing even the bathroom had been redone. He brushed the vomit and booze from his teeth and took one last deep breath before he headed out the door.

He approached the elevator, now a shining gold. The operator nodded at Tommy as he stepped in. "What floor, sir?"

"Uh, the lobby, please."

"Right away."

When he reopened the gate, Tommy barely had the wherewithal to thank him. It was as if the entire hotel had transformed. The low, rain-bloated ceilings that met Tommy when he arrived were completely gone, replaced by a high gold-leafed dome and bold, majestic columns. Grand chandeliers dripped light across shining surfaces, the cavernous space littered with ceramic sculptures, wall sconces, fountains, flowers —even the fireplace had been given a treatment with gold foil.

The hotel was in full swing, with bellhops pushing shining suit-case carts across burgundy carpet and marble floors while guests wove in and out as if it was just another day in an opulent New York City hotel. But this was not the city. Furthermore, they were all dressed as if it was right before the second war. But they weren't wearing costumes; the tweed suits and loose, low-waist dresses were brand new. The women even wore bobbed hair under hats, like in the pictures of Mami and her sisters when they were younger.

His panic returned, and he quickly located a place to hide—a line of telephone booths. He stumbled into one, hurrying to close the door before his frantic breaths betrayed him. What the hell was happening? Had he died in the tub—was this some kind of afterlife?

He closed his eyes, trying to gather his wits. When he was a boy, his brother used to sneak home comic books from school. He would wait until the whole house was asleep and sneak it into his room, pouring over the pictures in dim candlelight. His favorite ones were about time travel, where the heroes had to pretend to fit in so no one would catch on that they were imposters from the future.

That was it. He'd somehow traveled back in time. It was the only explanation. He didn't know exactly how or even when, but he definitely didn't want to raise any alarm. He looked down at his rolled-up slacks and suspenders and noticed how badly his hands shook. He needed to find some old-style clothes, but first, he needed a drink. And maybe a sandwich.

He rolled down his pants and slipped out of the phone booth, heading through the lobby and down the hall to what looked like a little diner with an open seating area. Couples were breakfasting around their tables, a few solo patrons holding up their newspapers while they drank their coffees. He noted a sign that said "Seat Your-self" and slid into a chair at one of the tables. There was a menu laid across the fancy tablecloth, and he picked it up to try to get a clue what year he was in.

His ears picked up music from a distant radio, reminding him of the songs he used to hear when he drove with Papi into the better parts of the city. The tinny sound of the radio spat out a man's voice: "You're the cream in my coffee, you're the lace in my shoe..." *Wait, I remember that song...*

It hit him. He'd gone back thirty years. He was in the 1920s.

"Hello, sir. What can I get you this afternoon?" A pleasant-faced waiter appeared in front of him.

"A gin–" Stories of the Prohibition days flashed in his mind. "A coffee, please. But if you can make it Irish, even better."

The waiter smiled, catching his drift. "Don't worry, sir, we are not a dry establishment. We will take care of whatever you need. May I offer you a proper whisky with today's special?"

"Yes, thank you." Tommy glanced down at the menu. "A deli sandwich sounds great."

"Excellent. I will be right back with your beverage."

Tommy exhaled and sat back in his seat. So far, so good.

He looked around the room, marveling at the gorgeous interior. If this was an accurate representation of what the hotel once was, whoever had let it go to hell deserved to be hanged. He didn't even want to start thinking about what he was going to do now. If it was 1920, that means he was only a child. That also meant... Mami was still alive.

"Hello, there."

Tommy realized he'd been staring in the direction of a well-dressed man reading a newspaper. "Oh, sorry. Got lost in my thoughts."

"Not to worry, old boy." The man chuckled as he neatly folded his paper. "I haven't seen you around before. Have you recently joined the 27 Club?"

Tommy felt his stomach sink. He hadn't had time to think about a cover story. "Nah, I'm just passing through."

The man didn't blink. He wore a fake smile, his gray eyes boring into Tommy's. "I see. Well, I do hope you'll join us for the New Year's Ball tonight."

Tommy couldn't hold in his surprise. "New Year?"

The man laughed pleasantly. "Well, yes. It's New Year's Eve, is it not?"

Tommy pulled himself together. "Well, as I said, I'm just passing through. Stuck here with the winter weather and all. I didn't bring anything formal with me."

"Nonsense. You must meet the hotel owner, Harold Dobby. He insists that all guests, new and regular, enjoy their experience here. Lord knows we paid a fortune to indulge in his Fountain of Youth." The man winked at him.

"I have a suit you can borrow," he continued. "My son is about your height. Oliver?" he called behind him.

The waiter from earlier appeared, tray in hand.

"Oliver, can you have one of my suits delivered to this fine chap at Room..."

The waiter didn't miss a beat. "Tommy Hawkins is in Room 218, sir."

Tommy stared, speechless.

"Excellent. Have one of my boy's suits delivered to Mr. Hawkins in Room 218 as soon as possible." The man took one last sip of his coffee and stood, tucking his paper under his arm. He walked over to a dumbfounded Tommy and stuck out his hand. "The name's Rockefeller."

Tommy's already-stuck words wedged themselves deeper into his throat as he shook the man's hand. The man didn't seem to mind, however, patting the shoulder of the waiter and disappearing into the swarm of bustling bodies.

The waiter went to Tommy's table and removed a short glass of gin and a cup of water from his tray.

"Oh, I don't need a chaser."

"Nonsense. The water here comes from our very own natural springs. They are world-renowned for their properties of healing and renewal. It's the reason Meadowbrook consistently operates at full capacity."

"Thank you," Tommy said. "Say, how did you know which room I'm in?"

"Why the ledger, sir. From when you checked in."

Tommy forced a smile. "Of course. Thank you, Mr. Oliver."

"Of course, sir."

Tommy watched him leave before taking down the gin and promptly whistling. It was some of the best he'd had in a long time. He let the taste of juniper linger on his tongue for a minute before sipping the water. Though he was quite sure that the waiter was feeding him a bunch of hooey, the water actually tasted delicious.

While the gin worked to soothe his nerves, he took a minute to weigh out his options. If he did drive back to Mami, would he run into his younger self? Would he even be able to get a car to come up here in the winter? He had no idea what the rules were for time travel, but he didn't want to mess anything up. All he knew was he wanted to see her one more time.

No longer hungry—he never ate when he had booze in his stomach—he stood to head to this room. He searched his pockets as he walked, glad to see he still held the gold key marked 218. He entered the gold elevator across the room, looking up to see a different smiling operator. It took him a moment to realize he had entered the wrong one. "Wait—"

"Hold the car, please!"

The elevator operator hurried to comply as the most beautiful woman Tommy had ever seen stepped into the car. Bright eyes peeked out from under short black curls held captive by a cloche hat, the fabric of her skirt hanging loose around slender legs ending in small heels. She started to politely step to the back of the car when Tommy's presence caught her attention.

"Are you new?" she asked.

Tommy stumbled over his words, finding himself lost in her eyes. "Something like that."

"New as in, you just arrived, or new as in, this is the first time I'm seeing you." A strange look had taken over her gentle, heart-shaped face, one Tommy couldn't place.

"Uh, I'm not sure what to say, miss."

She exchanged a look with the operator. "Jenkins, please take us straight up to four so I can introduce him to Harold."

The operator nodded and shut the gold-brushed gate. He pressed the uppermost, unmarked button, and the elevator lurched.

"Harold is the owner of the hotel, correct?" Tommy asked.

The woman nodded and then gestured with her eyes to the operator, whose back was turned. "We can talk more when we arrive," she said lightly.

They rode in silence as the car lumbered up the shaft, stopping at the top floor with a mechanical groan. The operator moved to re-open the gates, and the woman handed him a dollar from her slender purse.

"Thank you, Miss Olivia." He gave her a mock bow. "See you tonight."

Tommy followed her into a hallway much more opulent than the wing he was in. For one, it opened into its own lobby, and secondly, it housed a four-spout marble fountain at its center. Its blue-green marble gleamed in the dim light of a low-hanging chandelier, four beautiful mermaids smiling at him as they tipped their basins. The detail that went into sculpting each of their faces did not escape him, reminding him of statues from church.

"Follow me," the woman said over the rushing water. She didn't wait for a response, heading down the long corridor of regularly marked doors until she hit a bend where there were only two: one marked 419 and one right next to it that had been labeled, curiously enough, 502. She pushed her key into the lock and opened it to reveal a mini-staircase.

"This is the Northeast Penthouse, where I stay," she explained. She started up the stairs, offering a view Tommy struggled not to stare at.

"Will I be meeting your husband?" he asked uncomfortably, following her up with his eyes diverted.

"Harold is *not* my husband," she said in disgust from above. "And no, we must speak before he gets here."

Before Tommy had time to consider the implications of a strange woman inviting him into the room she shared with the hotel owner, he reached the top. Amazed that such a large space was so artfully concealed, he realized the stairs continued to yet another level, which he assumed was the bedroom. He stood now in an opulent parlor painted light purple. Light streamed in from an enormous bay window where he could see miles of snow-capped pines.

Olivia walked over to a nearby decanter and poured a drink into one of the crystal glasses.

He went to thank her, but she took her drink herself. Then she slammed down the glass and poured another.

"How much do you know?" she asked.

"Pardon?"

She handed him the glass, and he could see lines of exhaustion on her face. "What year did you come from?"

She knew.

Something in her eyes told him he could be truthful. "I checked in at the Meadowbrook Hotel in 1951," he replied. "It was falling apart; I never even heard of it before the operator suggested it."

She exhaled, leaning back against the counter. "That's not too far off. We're in 1927 right now. Well, forever, to be exact. We don't have much time, though, so I have to explain things quickly. What is your name?"

He took a sip of his drink, glad it was gin. Her lipstick had left a ring around the glass, and he could taste waxy cherry. He wondered if that's what it would taste like if he kissed her—juniper and cherry. He cleared his throat. "Tommy. Tommy Hawkins."

"Wait, Tommy Hawkins? As in Rockin' Tommy Hawkins?" She looked mystified. "The rising star who committed suicide in his thirties? You threw yourself from the balcony of a...hotel." She went back to the decanter, poured and housed another drink.

"Careful there, sweetheart or you won't make it to your party tonight."

"I'm from 1985," she said with her back turned. "I have no idea how long I've been here, trapped in time. We do not age if we stay in the same year over and over again. I could be the age I was before—thirty-one—or I could be eighty-five. I have no idea. There are no calendars, and I stopped making marks on the wall."

Tommy frowned, letting her words settle over him. "Why don't you just leave the hotel?"

She met his eyes. "I can't. Harold has the entire place heavily manned by security. Every hall, every room, every car is under his control. Somehow, long ago, he figured out what this place was and how to use it to his advantage. I have no idea how old he is or where he even comes from. All I know is that he controls the time travel within the hotel. Say, how did you jump?"

"Jump?"

"Travel."

He thought of the bathtub and cleared his throat. "Well, Ms. Olivia, I tried to off myself in the tub, and I woke up on the floor in my hotel room bathroom in a different time."

Her eyes widened. "You traveled through the water?"

"I suppose I did. Are there other ways?"

"Oh, yes. Certain stairwells and entryways will pop you somewhere else without having to almost die. But like I said, Harold keeps those heavily guarded. As he does the lower floor baths."

"Do you mind if I smoke? This is a lot to take in."

"Only if you give me one."

Tommy obliged, and they moved to a sitting room, where she sank gently down into one of the chairs.

Tommy followed suit. "So 1985, huh? What's life like in the future?"

She inhaled from her cigarette. "Well, women have more power. In my old life, I was a respected journalist for The New York Times. But I had an accident and came to Meadowbrook for a rest. They marketed it to the wealthy as a quiet retreat where you won't be bothered. But Harold took a shine to me immediately since I look almost identical to his precious Lisette. Before I could even figure out what was happening, he popped me in those damn baths. Now, here I am."

Tommy frowned. "So where is this Harold?"

"Traveling, of course. He has to, to keep this place in operation. He is quite skilled in the art of talking rich folks out of their money. He also has to ensure this place keeps standing through the other timelines. It's complicated."

"Sounds like it." Tommy polished off the gin. He was finally feeling like himself again, though he wished he'd eaten that sandwich. "Why are you telling me all this?"

"You came here by accident. I thought it might be best to give you the truth before Harold tells you his version. I won't be here after tonight."

"You plan to escape?"

"Every year on New Year's Eve, Harold throws a huge ball for the 27 Club. They are an elite group of millionaires from all over the world, all in different stages of life, who have paid to stay here, perpetually stuck in 1927. When life was good, they say. They never age, and they never die. They simply live in perpetual opulence and luxury, without a care in the world, while the rest of the world continues to move on without them." She exhaled and let the cigarette fall with a hiss into her near-empty glass.

"After the party and before the clock strikes midnight, Harold leads us all to the baths underground, where Harold performs a 'baptism.' We each sink into the water, and right before we drown, we are transported back to the beginning of the year. Sort of like how you did in the bathtub."

"Why can't you go back to 1985?"

"It doesn't work like that. Portals can go to any point in time, and there is no control over them. Harold is the only one who has ever figured out their pattern."

"So if you or I ever say, try to off ourselves, who knows where we'd end up?"

"Correct. As I said, Harold has the known portals heavily guarded, but the curious thing about the hotel is that she will create them when and where she sees fit. Several guests have accidentally found open portals and have never returned. Harold warns everyone about the implications of such a thing. You could get trapped in a time when no one knows who you are. Or worse, you could meet yourself from the future. When that happens, one of you will instantly die."

Tommy went quiet for a minute, thinking how strange it would be to see oneself. He shivered. "So how does all this work? What makes it possible? Feels like I'm stuck in a comic book."

"Harold believes it's the water from sacred springs. He creates elixirs from it, which he calls the Fountain of Youth. But I think the hotel itself is a liminal space that time cannot touch. Something is wrong here, which makes time able to be manipulated."

"If we can't time-hop safely, how do you plan to escape?"

She smiled, her blue eyes sparkling. "When everyone is at the ball, laughing and cheering immortality with their glasses of champagne, I will be burning this motherfucker to the ground."

He was taken aback for a minute at her peculiar language, and then he laughed. "Well, I guess that takes care of things, now doesn't it? So again, why tell me all this?"

"Because you didn't mean to end up here either. It's still 1927, and you're not Tommy Hawkins yet. You are still Tomas Hernandez, a little boy from Spanish Harlem."

"How—how did you know my name?"

"I told you. I used to be a journalist, and you are a famous musician from the fifties. Everyone knows your story in my time. How you were raised in poverty and found fame and fortune young. How you used to drink..." She trailed off uncomfortably. "You're in books and magazines—in fact, you were one of the first inducted into The Rock and Roll Hall of Fame."

"The what Fame?"

"And Tomas will still grow up to be Tommy Hawkins. But you, as you exist right now in this place, can continue going on as your own person. You can do whatever you want—you are completely free."

"That's why you want to escape."

She nodded. "The 1920s looks good on me. I have no children and no man worth finding again. I stashed enough money to get through the Depression and World War II when they come. I plan to head into the mountains to Canada and do as I please. You could do the same."

Tommy studied her face. If he left, he could see Mami. Papi would even be alive. He could give them money or get them out of the old tenement before Papi's accident. Maybe he wouldn't even have to die. "Alright, then. Tell me the plan."

———

Pleasantly buzzed, but not drunk, Tommy straightened his tie in the mirror. He had tried his best to imitate the old style of hair, but although his skin and eyes were light enough that he passed for white, his thick hair let it be known he was Puerto Rican. He stood back to straighten the tuxedo Rockefeller had sent him, which was a surprisingly good fit. A damn Rockefeller, he thought, shaking his head. He wondered what other famous names he'd see tonight, all paying their way for eternal life.

He took another drink from the bottle he'd lifted from Harold and Olivia's quarters and lit another cigarette. He grabbed the accompanying top hat on the way out, whistling as he strolled back down the hall. Either it was the drink, the water, or Olivia's pretty blue eyes, but something in the air made him feel light again.

The lobby swarmed with hotel patrons dressed in their finest, heading to the Golden Ballroom at the furthest point in the hotel. Aptly named, the almost obnoxious amount of shimmering gold accents created a blinding effect with its decorative tinsel, a huge sign boasting, "Happy New Year!" draped across one of the mirrored walls. Tommy slipped in and around dozens of swirling tuxedo-clad men and pearl-dripping women, noticing the chandeliers reflecting in the polished dance floor. Though it was dark outside, the back patio had been lit, illuminating a gentle snowfall.

Across the room, a band labored on stage with a stuffy ballroom tune. He suddenly wondered what it must feel like to be trapped playing music for rich folks who ought to be dead for eternity. Did they pay their way to be here, too?

"Mr. Hawkins!"

A booming voice interrupted his thoughts.

Tommy turned to see a bespectacled man with outstretched arms heading his way. He was grinning, a cigar in one hand and a glass of scotch in the other. For someone of such small stature, he walked with an exaggerated gait as if he were the most important man alive, a rich purple bow tie protruding from his black pin-stripe suit. He stuck the cigar between his teeth and shook Tommy's hand. "Welcome to Meadowbrook."

"Nice to meet you, Mr. Dobby."

"Call me Harold, please."

A crowd of tuxedoed men had appeared around him, adding smoke from their own respective cigars. One of them handed a cigar to Tommy, another offering a lit match. Tommy took a puff, impressed that here, even the cigars tasted good.

"My wife mentioned we had a true star in our midst," Harold told the men behind him. "From the 50s, no?"

"Ah yes, that's correct," Tommy stammered.

"Well, not anymore!" one of the men laughed.

"Time has no meaning for the 27 Club!" another said, lifting his glass.

"Forever 27!" The rest of the men cheered in unison, clinking their glasses together in a toast.

Harold, still grinning, led Tommy away from the crowd. "I hate to talk business at a party, but I'm assuming you arranged payment with Ms. Helen."

Tommy scanned the room for Olivia, but she was nowhere to be found. "Actually, no. I found my way here by accident."

Harold's beady gray eyes widened behind his glasses. "By accident? Are you not the Rockin' Tommy Hawkins?"

"It's not that I don't have the money," Tommy stammered, suddenly uncomfortable. There was something not quite right in the man's eyes, like they were a little too big, kind of like his Cheshire cat smile. "I came to this hotel for another reason—I didn't mean to come here."

Harold's smile dropped. "Who brought you here?"

"No one—"

Harold squeezed his arm. "Was it that wretched Cindy?" he said between clenched teeth. "Or that blasted Matthew?" His eyes had darkened.

"No, I—it was the bathtub."

He paused and deflated as he considered his words. "We need to talk. Right this way, to my office."

"What about your party?"

He waved his hand dismissively. "Nothing begins or ends here without me."

Tommy followed him as he wove through the crowd to the hall, stopping every few feet to shake a hand and offer a smile. He saw a few familiar faces in the sea of rich, white men and women, but no one seemed to recognize him at all. Though Olivia had no trouble placing his identity, a rock musician seemed below the radar of the world's elite.

Harold ducked down a short hallway, past the front desk and what Tommy assumed was the rest of the administrative offices, to a full suite with gold trim that clashed against its lavender walls. It was the exact opposite of the executive suites Tommy had seen in Hollywood.

Harold closed the door behind him, gesturing for him to sit. "I'm sure the bright colors might seem a little odd to you, but I like things to stay bright. I once ran a cancer hospital here at Meadowbrook and decided to bring the color scheme back here. I could never understand why hospitals were always so bland and monochrome. Sick people need color and excitement. It promotes wellness."

Harold went behind his desk and poured a glass of water from a crystal carafe, which he pushed Tommy's way. He poured himself a glass and raised it in a mock toast. "I'm sure my wife explained to you all about the water here."

Tommy choked.

"No worries," Harold said, leaning back in his chair. "She'll be dealt with appropriately. Told you all that horseshit about being trapped here, did she? She's a complete loon. I tried everything to rehabilitate her, even giving her a nice place to stay. My old penthouse! But she won't cease her attempts at violence. I should have left her in the psych ward. But I have a big ol' heart, I can't help it."

"She said you two weren't married."

He laughed and pulled a paper from his desk.

Tommy looked down to see a marriage certificate with both their names printed clear as a bell. They'd been married well before

1927, and both the judge and minister had signed it. So Olivia was not at all what she seemed.

"I love the woman, don't get me wrong. But she's tried to set this place on fire too many times to count. I can't have her upsetting the folks who pay good money to be here. Not only that, one day, she'll end up killing someone innocent."

"So you travel through time here?"

Harold smiled. "Crazy, I know. It was crazy to me, too, until I realized what a gift this place is. It is a true miracle."

"Do you keep people here forever?"

"Despite what Olivia has told you, everyone who comes is free to leave. But who would? Who would choose to grow old, wither, and die?"

Tommy grew quiet, thinking of the tub. "I wanted to die. That's why I came here."

Harold nodded, his eyes swimming with sympathy. "Is it the drink?"

Tommy realized he'd been wrong about Harold. He'd met Harold's stage self, the man he had to pretend to be around others. Tommy could relate; he had a visage too. But here, away from the crowd, Harold was kind and soft, as if he could see right through Tommy, but didn't judge what he saw. Two equals.

Tommy sighed. "It's all of it."

"Well, Tomas—can I call you by your real name?"

"Yeah."

"Tomas, you are tired of your mask. Of the facade you put on in front of others. Your entire life, you've been wearing a mask. Whether it was to protect you as a poor kid on the streets or as an adult navigating the music industry, who never quite fit in. You've worn it to the point of overuse. The alcohol won't even keep it intact. It's time to let it go. It's time to be free."

Tommy looked down, surprised to feel tears welling in the corners of his eyes.

"Many folks don't know this, but I am actually a doctor, Tomas. I can help you. And I can do something that no other doctor can do—I can offer you immortality. Olivia thinks she will be free if she leaves this hotel, but true freedom is never having to die."

Tommy looked into his eyes. The darkness he'd seen earlier was gone. He thought of Olivia, how she had said she had nothing left to miss. He thought of May and the empty, childless house they lived in. She'd be better off without him.

There was a knock at the door. "Sir, it's nearing midnight," a man called.

"Coming, Oliver." Harold stood. "Give it some thought, Tomas. The decision is yours. I can pop you back to 1951 if you'd like. Just let me know. Then, you can either drink yourself to death or go back to your life as a star. But I would suggest staying out of the water this time." He winked at him.

Tommy stood, straightening his jacket.

"Ready for a New Year's Eve to remember?"

Tommy smiled despite himself. For the first time in a very long time, things didn't seem so heavy.

They headed back through the throng of glittering bodies, and Harold made his way to the stage. Tommy grabbed a glass—this time, of water. The crowd began to cheer as they watched Harold's short figure jog up the stage steps, thrilled to see their host.

He grinned as he approached the microphone, adjusting his purple tie as he tapped it a few times. "Is this thing on?" he joked.

The crowd rippled with laughter. Tommy felt himself being squeezed in by the people around him, but not unpleasantly. More like a warm embrace, a feeling of belonging. Maybe the hotel had brought him here. Hadn't Olivia referred to it as a 'she'? Maybe she'd brought him home.

Harold cleared his throat as a spotlight snapped on, bathing him in light. His voice boomed through the microphone. "Welcome, my friends, to another Year 1927!"

The crowd erupted in cheers as the band started back up. Tommy joined the sounds of jubilation as champagne splashed all around him.

"Another year has passed," Harold continued when the noise

had died down, "and I again find myself honored to share this new life with all of you. This hotel and its sacred waters are a true gift, one that allows us to spit in the face of death—to defy God himself!"

The crowd cheered again.

"We are the gods here, ladies and gentlemen!" Harold cried.

The crowd roared. All the classy decorum applied earlier had been lost to their passion. It was as if, at that moment, they remembered that they had all escaped the thing that every human feared, and the air sizzled with excitement. They were no longer bound by death—they were free.

"Ladies and Gentleman of the 27 Club, midnight grows near. But first, we have a little unpleasant business to attend to."

"Boo!"

"I know, I know," Harold said with a patient smile. "I do hate to ruin a good party. But as much as I try to please you all, there are some here who do not want this gift. They fight it tooth and nail. Now, I know our security precautions may seem extreme, but I take your protection very seriously. And tonight, my efforts have served us well. The good men of the Meadowbrook Security discovered an attempted arson."

The purple curtain behind him pulled back, revealing none other than Olivia. Dressed in a feathered headband and pearls, she looked as beautiful as ever, though her face was twisted in anger. Held captive by two uniformed men, she was pushed forward until she reached center stage, where a smaller spotlight settled on her.

"Now you all know my wife, Olivia."

"I'm not your wife—" she began, but Harold spoke louder.

"Most of you have been with me since the beginning and have known how I tried to give Olivia anything she could ever want here at Meadowbrook. Heartbroken after I lost my beloved Lisette, I fell hard."

"Lisette was a first-class woman," a man said wistfully from beside Tommy.

"But Olivia does not want this life. Olivia wants to try to time hop on her own."

Olivia attempted to protest, but it was no use. The crowd was restless, volatile even, eager to see what their host had planned. Tommy thought of coming to her aid, but for what? Did he really know her? Why would she try to ruin such an amazing place? The more he considered it, the more it seemed she didn't belong here.

And he did.

"Olivia will not be joining our New Year's festivities. Instead, she will remind us all what happens when we try to time-hop alone. Now, I have been transparent with you all since the beginning—I have warned you that time travel is not without rules. Long ago, I figured them out, and I go to great lengths to keep us all safe. I make sure our needs are met. But time travel is dangerous. Let us never forget Time's power!"

The curtain rustled and moved, and this time, a coffin was wheeled forward.

The crowd replied in murmurs of excitement.

Tommy felt as if he should have been horrified to hear someone beating their fists at its lid from inside, but he felt nothing. He couldn't even see Olivia's face anymore. He took another sip of water, wondering what would come next.

Harold stepped over to the coffin, prepared to open it. "Let this be a lesson," he cried. "That we do not tempt our fate with Time!"

With gusto, the coffin opened, and the crowd gasped as Olivia —an Olivia from another time—stumbled out onto the stage floor.

The entire room went silent as she scrambled to her feet.

Tommy watched in frozen awe as the Olivia he'd just met hours ago met herself from some different time. They stared at each other for only a moment before both of them realized what was happening. He thought he would hear a shriek as their mouths mirrored each other in a perfect 'O', but there was nothing.

Nothing but a loud pop as one of their beautiful heads exploded, splattering Harold, the crowd, and Tommy with horrible pink, red, and purple gore.

CHAPTER SEVEN

Michael, 1946

Wind tossed Michael's hair as he rolled down the window of his brand-new Bentley to flick his cigarette. Without missing a beat, he fumbled for another, keeping the match flame steady as he maneuvered the car up and down the winding country roads.

He sighed out the smoke. He was tired, the kind of tired that no amount of black coffee could fix. He'd been traveling for hours in the summer heat, wondering how he got talked into another one of Ralph's crazy ideas. The problem with Ralph was that no matter how crazy they were, his ideas always produced a gold mine. Michael couldn't afford to ignore him. Especially not after that crazy Doris broad claimed she was knocked up. If she wasn't bullshitting him, he'd have *another* secret set of mouths to feed—because if he knew women, which he did, she'd want monthly shut-up money. He scowled as he loosened his necktie, wondering how much farther up the damn mountain he'd have to go.

Like a gift from Heaven, the colossal hotel emerged from its perch on the mountaintop. Why someone would even build such a heap in the middle of the country was beyond him. There was no railroad that ran anywhere near the town, if it could be called a town. All Michael saw, after miles of farmland, was one dilapidated square with one petrol station, a town hall, and a run-down general store.

He squinted to get a better look, discovering it was two full wings wide with spires that threatened to block out what little blue sky the trees left open. He shook his head, increasing speed. He couldn't wait to hear what Ralph had to say about this. Bringing him to Dracula's castle, what a racket.

Michael soon learned the grounds were fenced in by stone walls with sharp ironwork at the top. Overgrown brush and stringy vines crawled down them both, letting him know the place hadn't been maintained in years. He reached the front gate, which had been left open, and read the iron letters at the top. He laughed, shaking his head in disbelief.

With a screech of his tires, he roared up the driveway, sending billowing dirt clouds behind him. Bugs splattered his windshield while unseen critters scurried back into the tall grass and weeds that surrounded him. Through the unkempt bushes, he saw Ralph's car up ahead. As soon as he could make out the skinny Italian leaning against the hood, smoking a Lucky, he accelerated once more, aiming his screeching stop so that dust would kick up in his face.

Ralph spit and shook his shirt before giving him a look that clearly read: *asshole*. He put both hands out. "Really?"

"*Me* really?" Michael slammed the car door behind him. "*You* really. Meadowbrook Place for Wellness? You got me comin' out to the middle of nowhere to a fucking hospital?"

"Relax," Ralph soothed, giving him the sideways grin he always gave when he was about to convince someone to do something for him. It still worked on Michael, and he'd known him since they were kids. "You're gonna love this place. Mouse!" he called.

From around the bend appeared Ralph's lawyer and accountant, a short, wiry guy with glasses and a nose that overwhelmed his narrow face. Though he could shoot a man point blank without so much as a blink, he spent his normal hours nervous and twitchy. In grade school, it had earned him the name Mouse, something that never died, no matter how old they all got. Michael always liked him; no matter what Ralph had going on, Mouse kept his books tight. They all took care of each other, like family.

"Hey, Mouse."

"Hey, Mikey," Mouse squeaked. "Whatya think about this place?"

"A fuckin' hospital, Mouse?"

"Nah, it was a luxury hotel first. Some quack bought it a few years back and turned it into an experimental cancer hospital. He got arrested for fraud, and the place shut down. No one wants to touch it."

Michael sighed. "But Ralph Galzano does."

"There used to be a railroad that ran up here, and all the richest folks came to stay," Mouse continued, looking up at the building as he spoke.

Michael followed his gaze. The building itself was pretty impressive, though several of its windows had been shattered, the double porches were caving in, and the roof was in bad need of repair. He tried to picture what it looked like when it was first built when the limestone was freshly laid and the wood clean.

Ralph grinned, looking like a little kid on Christmas morning. "Come on, let's go inside."

He led them up the steps under the wide covered porch to the front archway. Michael noticed several rocking chairs had been left behind, their white paint chipped as they swayed in the summer breeze.

"Keep in mind this place was left how the quack painted it," Ralph called from inside, his voice echoing. "Guy had horrible taste."

Their footsteps crunched broken glass and debris as they entered the main lobby. Michael saw exactly what his friend meant; what should have been marble floors, strong Greek pillars, and elaborate woodwork had been ruined by bright purples, pinks, and yellows, geometric shapes, and obnoxious murals. Over the back porch archway were the faded words, *"If you cure after others fail, you're a quack!"*

"Christ, what a nightmare," he muttered.

"A total quack, right?" Ralph chuckled. "People actually fell for that shit. Had them eating out of the palm of his hand."

"This hotel sits right near several hot springs," Mouse interjected. "That's why they built this hotel in the first place. The quack saw an opportunity and seized it."

"Like we will." Ralph said with bright eyes.

Michael threw his hands up in alarm. "Whoa, I ain't running no hospital."

"Mouse, show him the plans."

The tiny man slammed his briefcase on the oversized front desk. It looked to Michael as if it had been made from mahogany, a real piece of craftsmanship. Shame it was covered in an inch of dust. Mouse unlatched the briefcase and pulled out a rolled sheet of paper, sending slivers of glass and debris trickling to the floor as he cleared the way to unroll it.

Michael peered over his shoulder.

From the floorplans, he saw the hotel sat on twenty-seven acres and boasted over thirty rooms, with three elevators and a basement full of swimming pools. Mouse had attached a few photographs showing the original interior with chandeliers and shining gold fixtures.

"We fix it up and re-open the hotel, like a luxurious escape," Ralph's voice came beside him. "People don't want to think of the war no more, they want an escape, a place to forget and spend money. We run it like the casinos but with fresh air and special water. Call it something real fancy like, 'A Castle in the Air High Atop the Mountains.' Then we set up a wing for our special clientele and give 'em booze and broads."

"Making it a perfect spot to clean money."

Ralph offered another grin. "And it's the perfect spot for us to clean money."

Michael sighed, studying the plans. "I assume Johnny approves?"

"He says it's our project, so it's up to you. I talked him into giving me a loan, though. We're getting the place for a fucking steal, Mikey."

Michael surveyed the foyer. Before he got into the business with the guys, he loved to build. Something about using his hands to create; putting in a hard day's work felt so rewarding. He knew he could lead the project; he'd oversaw dozens of projects for them, including Johnny's casinos. He thought about his wife, the kids, then Linda, Betty, and now Doris, and their kids. He really could use the money.

"Alright, alright."

Ralph threw his arms around him, and they were suddenly young boys again, talking smack on the corner of Mulberry Street about how one day they were gonna get out of the neighborhood and make something of themselves.

"The realtor should be here any moment," Mouse said, checking his watch. "You guys wanna see the rest of the place?"

He led them onward through the lobby, carpeted with an ugly purple that had begun to grow mold. It led all the way to the stairwell, and as they ascended, Michael looked up to see a giant split where part of the ceiling fell through. "Gotta get a quote on the roof first thing," he remarked. He ran his fingers along the painted wood railing, the thick white paint peeling away to reveal more gorgeous carved mahogany. The urge to drop everything and strip it was strong.

"Excuse me, gentlemen?"

The men paused.

Standing at the door was a man wearing a suit and thick glasses, holding his own attache case.

"You must be Dobby." Mouse headed back down the stairs to shake his hand. Ralph and Michael followed casually behind him.

The man nodded and stuck out his hand. "Yes, sir. I'm from the Meadowbrook Springs Investment Company."

"Joseph Bertelone. I represent the interests of Ralph Galzano."

Michael hid a smile. He loved it when Mouse got all proper when he did his business. So did Ralph; gone was the boyish charmer who had just hugged him. In his place was a man with a steely gaze, carved out of the streets of New York City.

"Great to meet you." The man offered his hand, but Ralph didn't shake it.

"I've spoken to my associates, and we want to make the deal," Ralph said immediately. "My accountant here can write you up a check."

The realtor sputtered. "Don't you want to take a tour?"

"Nah, we're gonna gut it out and fix it up real nice," Ralph told him. "Doesn't matter how the quack left it."

The realtor twitched. "Well, alright then. I'll draw up the paperwork as soon as I get back to the office. We should have it to you within a few days—"

A roll of approaching thunder interrupted him.

"Can't we just sign it now?" Ralph asked. "We gotta get back home. We're not from around these parts."

The realtor looked nervous, and Michael almost felt bad for the guy. He really had no idea the type of people he was dealing with. One false move, they'd find him face down in the pond.

"Well, I can probably draft you something tonight if you gentlemen don't mind staying for the evening. The company has kept the administrative office attached to the hotel in operation throughout the years; the rooms are all in good shape with electricity and gas."

Michael frowned.

"You gotta be kiddin' me," Ralph muttered, echoing his annoyance.

"That would be great, Mr. Dobby," Mouse said. "We appreciate your hospitality."

"Look, you guys don't need me to stay for the papers, right?" Michael cut in. "Cuz I'm starved, and Maria's making ziti—"

There was another loud boom of thunder above, which promptly released torrents of rain. They slammed into the ceiling, funneling down from the crack Michael noted in the ceiling. The men scrambled to get out of its way when a figure shielded by a cloak rushed into the lobby.

Before anyone could react, a woman's voice rang out. "It's a damn monsoon out there!" She removed the soaking cloak to reveal a beautiful, though flustered, face. Rain soaked her dark hair, sending streams between the kind of blue eyes that got Michael into trouble. But before he could say anything, the realtor broke in.

"I told you that you shouldn't wait out there," he chided her, not unlike a father to his daughter. "But don't fret about the rain, dearest. We're going to stay the night at the administrative wing with these fine gentlemen."

She appraised them all with fiery, annoyed eyes and a lifted eyebrow. Her sass was pure Italian, Michael thought before catching himself. The last thing he needed was more drama with another broad...but the legs under her pencil skirt let him know it was going to be hard to control himself.

"You'll have to excuse my secretary, Ms. Lisette," Harold addressed the three of them with a nervous laugh. "She forgets her place sometimes."

"She can interrupt us anytime she likes." Michael grinned.

"Wherever we're headed, we should do so now," Mouse interrupted, gesturing to the crooked river forming in the purple carpet.

Lisette gave her wet cloak a shake and marched off, her shoes squelching in the soaked fabric.

Dobby scrambled to follow her. "Right this way, gentlemen."

Michael exchanged looks with an aggravated but defeated Ralph. "First dibs on the broad," he joked.

Ralph turned to Mouse. "This is fucking ridiculous."

"Like we haven't slept in worse places," Mouse reminded him. "You're getting too used to having money."

"Ain't no such thing."

"Come on, Ralph." Michael put a hand on his shoulder. "Ain't no driving in this mess anyhow."

They headed across the lobby, swerving around piles of rotting wood, glass, and the kind of plants that liked to sprout anywhere they fell. Michael looked to the right to see the ballroom, tree branches snaking through what must have been ornate windows. The way the wind hit made them look like arms fighting to come in.

The second lobby had been saved from deterioration, probably because it had been built later with better material. It had the same ridiculous patterns as the main part of the hotel but with far less pomp. Dobby bypassed the old Otis elevator to a door at the far end. He fetched a key from his pocket and turned the knob.

"I don't remember this building in the plans," Mouse muttered as they followed him in.

Dobby lit up. "You have the original floor plans?"

"One of your associates mailed them to me when we inquired about the property," Mouse replied.

Michael smiled to himself. Inquired. Mouse was back to business.

"How wonderful," Dobby remarked. He felt around the wall for a light switch, and the lights flickered before they flooded a clean, modern space free of mold and debris. Michael saw a kitchenette not far from where they stood, as well as a couple of open offices nearby. To the left, beyond an unimpressive common room, was a line of doors with black painted numbers.

"The original wing was the servant's quarters for the grand Meadowbrook Estates Hotel," Dobby told Mouse. "When a fire decimated the east wing, they used this one for the main lodging. They turned it into a dormitory when Meadowbrook became a finishing school for girls, but that only lasted a few years. The most recent owner, the one who founded Meadowbrook Place for Wellness, turned it into his own living quarters. He wanted to live next to his patients to give them the best care possible. He had the space we're standing in built to house the staff; at one time, Meadow-brook was home to over a hundred souls."

"I'm sure they all got the hell outta dodge once the quack got arrested," Michael muttered.

He thought he saw Dobby twitch again.

"There is a kitchenette down the hall," Dobby continued, "and every room has its own bathroom. You can have whatever room you'd like except the upst—"

Lisette breezed past them all to the stairs, letting it be known that she would, indeed, be taking that one. From above, Micheal heard the door slam shut.

"I'll draw up the papers for you by tomorrow morning," Dobby promised Mouse.

"Sounds good, Mr. Dobby." The men exchanged another firm handshake. "Thanks again."

Michael watched Dobby hurry up the stairs after his secretary and shook his head.

"Oh yeah, like you got room to judge." Ralph snorted beside him.

"Hey, now—"

"You gonna cook us some grub, Mouse?"

Mouse shook his head. "You boys are on your own. I'm fuckin' exhausted." He went over to one of the rooms and tried the door.

Michael and Ralph peeked in from behind him. It was as expected. It was the kind of bland hotel room you'd find anywhere along the state route. The men exchanged their typical "Goodnight, don't let the bed bugs bite your ass," and Michael headed to another room. He threw his hat across the room and flopped down onto the bed, which let out a rude squeak. Outside, the storm talked back, pattering rain down his window in between claps of thunder. Maria wasn't going to be pleased he had to stay out all night, but she'd be glad once he found out he didn't try to drive the new auto in a downpour. Women cared about money more than anything.

Michael sighed and fished out a smoke. Maria was a decent woman, old-school like his mother. He didn't deserve her and he knew it, but he was glad she'd been sucker enough to marry him before he messed up too bad. And not just with the other women. He was getting pretty deep into the business, too. It wasn't terrible; he knew exactly what to say and do to keep the boss happy and his reputation clean. But things were changing. It was only a matter of time before something happened, especially with Ralph's ambition. Michael's loyalty lay with his brothers above all else, and he hoped there'd never be a day where that was tested.

He sighed, wishing he wasn't alone in a boring hotel room with his thoughts. This was usually about the time when he'd find himself a call girl—or any girl willing—and distract himself for the night. Too bad that Lisette broad was taken—if she was really taken. He never had any issue taking away some guy's girl. Maybe he would sneak in and pay her a visit. He'd need a little liquid courage first; he probably had some left over in his flask in his glove box. Then it hit him.

He'd left his gun in the car.

Groaning, he hopped to his feet and grabbed his coat, praying the guys wouldn't hear him as he snuck out. The last thing he wanted to do was explain what a careless jackass he was. He'd never hear the end of it.

Thankfully, their little space was dark and still. He slipped out unnoticed, his shoes slipping and sliding on the soaked purple carpet as he tried to make it through the main lobby without getting soaked.

The wind screamed as he walked out the front door, and he pulled up the collar of his coat, bracing for a fight to the car.

"Hey, you shouldn't be in here."

Michael blinked, realizing there was a girl sitting on one of the old deck chairs, lazily rocking back and forth. Wrapped up in a thin but oversized housecoat, she peered at him through the smoke of her cigarette. He couldn't make out her features in the dark.

"Me? Who the hell are you?"

"Easy, pal. I just came out to watch the rain."

"My buddy came up here to buy this place. They didn't mention nothing about guests."

She shrugged, taking a slow drag. "The company selling to you still rents out the east wing for pennies. They said we can stay 'til the papers are signed."

"What the hell are you doing out here? It's a fucking doozy out there."

She wiggled a hydroponic needle between her fingers. "Don't matter to me. I was just about to get high."

Michael snorted. "You couldn't have picked somewhere less wet?"

She laughed. "I get sick of my room sometimes. Hey, you up for a drink? I have an unopened bottle of vodka."

Michael thought about the boring room he'd just left. Thoughts of Maria. His stomach growled. "Booze is great, but it'd be even better if you had some food."

"Lucky for you, I got both." She climbed to her feet. She was a tiny thing, drowning in all that fabric. "Follow me."

Michael obliged, dodging the leaky parts of the porch as he pictured Ralph's reaction when he told him he met some junkie broad on the front porch and went straight up to her room. He wondered how many drinks it would take to get her to wiggle out of that housecoat and bathrobe. She was tiny enough—two, maybe three? He licked his lips, hoping she'd put up a little fight.

They turned the corner, and he was smacked with another rainy squall, forcing him to grab his hat. The surrounding trees thrashed, and she squealed as she darted into the hotel.

Michael couldn't see an inch in front of his face until she flipped on a flashlight, sending scant yellow light around youthful features and a mess of blonde hair. "You alright, big guy?"

"Yeah, I'm good." He couldn't see past the glow of the flashlight, but the east lobby smelled of old wood and stale air. Here, the ceiling did not leak.

"There's no electricity, so we gotta take the stairs," she

explained. "But it's only a couple floors—not too bad, I promise." She padded along the floor to the far end of the room.

Michael squinted as she opened the door to a stairwell which managed to be even darker than the lobby. "So you're really a squatter." He should have known.

"No one likes a judgmental bastard," she said playfully as she began to climb the stairs.

He chuckled. "I prefer Michael."

"No one likes a judgmental bastard, *Michael.*"

He heard the smile in her voice and couldn't help but do the same.

They reached the third floor when his bad knee started to ache, his daily reminder that he wasn't getting any younger. He paused to catch his breath as she effortlessly floated onward, like a ghost in all her loose beige fabric.

"Almost there," she called, finally pushing the door open to the fourth floor.

Michael pushed himself up one more flight and grimaced as he stepped onto the wet, squishy carpet, the smell of mildew and death assaulting his nose. He'd been wrong about the ceiling; rain gushed in from the spot where it had completely caved in, accumulating into an old fountain in the middle of the room. Green algae obscured most of its details, but from where he stood, it looked like there were sculptures of mermaids.

There was a shift and a crack, and another chunk of ceiling fell nearby, smashing into the floor with a resounding thud.

"Holy shit, is it safe to be here?" Michael didn't want to admit it, but he was rattled. No broad was worth almost dying for.

She laughed as she floated down the hall. "Aw, don't tell me you're scared," she taunted as she floated down the hall. She stopped at the end, where she shoved open a door marked 413.

Michael tentatively entered after her, letting the door clang shut as she flew around the room to light her candles. Soon, the dark room was bathed in flickering warmth.

He was surprised to see the room didn't look half bad, as if it'd been preserved while the rest of the hotel fell apart. Three floor-to-ceiling windows showed off a view he imagined would've been quite the sight had it not been night and blurred by sheets of rain.

He slumped down on the bed, watching as she removed her housecoat to finally reveal her petite figure. It was clad in nothing but a slip-dress, the outline of her nipples visible in the sheer fabric. She abruptly interrupted his goggling by ducking into the adjoining room. She returned with two dingy glasses and a bottle that she unceremoniously tossed his way. Then she fell into the chair nearest the window, retrieving her needle from the pocket of her housecoat.

Michael left the glasses on the bed and took a swig straight from the bottle. It was the cheap stuff, but on an empty stomach, it would do the job. "What's that in your hand anyway? That doesn't look like any junk I ever seen."

She looked up. "It's a concoction of barbiturates, herbs, and miracle water. I call it the Dobby Delight." She rotated her arms to show the track marks running up and down her skin. "Not good for the veins, but great for the brain."

Michael stared at her. "What's that mean?"

She giggled. "Nothing. Say, will you tell me what year it is?"

Michael took another gulp as she pushed the drugs into her vein. "You're that much of a druggie you don't know the year?"

She looked back at him with dreamy, glazed brown eyes. Apparently, the junk hit quick. "You're lucky I just took a hit, or I'd tear you a new one for that."

"Oh yeah?" He snorted. "You look about eighty pounds soaking wet."

"Eighty-*fiiive*," she joked in a slurred voice with a lopsided grin. Her teeth looked too good for a druggie, tall and polished white.

He took another sip of vodka. "'46."

Her eyes widened. "Ooo, I wonder if I'll meet June when she was young. Oh, wait, that might have been the fifties."

Michael squinted at her as the booze settled in, fuzzing up his brain. "You're a real crazy broad, you know that?"

"Who's crazier—the junkie in an old hotel or the gangster who followed her to her hotel room?"

At that, he laughed. "Alright, enough of the funny shit. Who else is here?"

She looked thoughtful. "Oh, there are so many now. Harold can't even keep track. Let's see—me, Olivia, June, P.J., Matthew... oh, and the rest of the 27 Club. I never see them, though. And, of course, Harold and Helen. Lisette is around, too, but she's always running around giving Harold hell. She's the one who got me these." She ran her tongue over her teeth. That was what was so strange about them—they were dentures.

"Wait, Listette?" Michael frowned. "And Harold, the realtor? They're in the other wing where me and my boys are staying."

The broad jumped to her feet. "She's here? Right now?"

"Yeah, her and that Harold guy."

"Oh shit, I gotta go."

"What do you mean, you gotta go?"

"Look, I'll be right back," she promised, clumsily climbing back into her housecoat. "There's food around here—help yourself to whatever you need."

"Now, wait just a minute—" But before he could reach up to grab her arm, she was gone.

Michael scowled, faced again with an empty room and an empty stomach that sloshed around cheap, rot-gut booze. He hoisted himself off the bed, determined at least to find a snack.

After sorting through piles of wrappers, empty bottles, and other weird druggie paraphernalia, he determined that whatever food she'd promised him had been a lie. Furious, he threw the half-empty bottle of vodka at the wall. He stood surprised when it did not shatter; instead, it sunk right into the wood. He squinted, realizing there was a hole in the wall that had been covered by wallpaper. He stuck his hand in and pulled out a handful of papers. He put his hand back in again and realized there was more, all covered in writing.

A flash of lightning streaked across the sky, throwing bright, angry light into the room. Michael fell back onto the bed, squinting to read the typewriter print.

November 13, 1992

I once was told the definition of insanity is doing the same thing repeatedly and expecting different results. I understand this because I do it every day. Load the typewriter with a fresh sheet of paper, expecting the words to come. But they never do. I'm worried they might not let me keep my type-writer unless I'm actively typing, so I've decided to create a journal. I can't say it will be very amusing, as I haven't kept a diary since I was a child, but I can say it beats my nightly pacing.

Micheal stared at the date, confused. Then he flipped to the next page, this one written in pen.

June 13, 1960?

I made it to 1960(?) through the stairwell portal: Meadowbrook Psychiatric Facility. Still no advance of my symptoms. I think Cindy is right; if we keep moving, we won't age or die. I will continue to leave these notes each time I hop so others can find me. I ran into a woman named June today who seemed to understand I was traveling but didn't reveal much. I plan to hang out here until I can meet Harold.

Another page, this time, in pencil.

May 12, 1938

Something is not right here. Harold is kind, but I

believe he suspects what we're doing. I am already registered as a patient here; some seem to do well, but others are deteriorating quickly. They disappear in the middle of the night. It will be harder for me to escape this one; they are watching my every move. I don't have a lot of time to write—I will try to write more later.

Another page, with no date, in a completely different hand-writing.

TIME IS IRRELEVANT. WE ARE THE IMMORTALS. OVER DEATH, WE WILL PREVAIL. ALL THOSE WHO SEEK—FIND THE DOORS MARKED WITH BLOOD.

Micheal dropped the pages as a shiver rolled down his spine. Outside, another bolt of lightning struck, this time hitting one of the trees. It caught fire, even in the pouring rain. He was getting the hell out of here—broad or no broad.

He marched back into the hallway, dodging and swerving his way back to the stairwell, cursing himself for not grabbing her flashlight. He could barely see beyond the lightning bolts that briefly illuminated the rubble. His heart raced more than he wanted to admit. Crazy bitch—he should have never followed her up there. When would he learn?

The stairwell was pitch black without his flowy tour guide, and he lit one of his matches with shaking fingers. It lasted for exactly one short stairwell. He continued to light them, one for each set of stairs until he saw they were about to run out. He frowned. After a full book of matches, he should have been where he was supposed to be.

Michael stopped to catch his breath, craning to see how long he'd been walking. The floors above him seemed endless. He licked lips gone dry with nerves and exertion, wishing he hadn't discarded that bottle. He was tired, hungry, and a little drunk, but as the last match went out, he saw a door with a weird crossed-out triangle symbol scratched on it. Maybe that was his floor, maybe it wasn't, but he had no other options. *I'm getting the hell outta this stairwell.*

Michael threw himself forward, and the door popped right open, spitting him out on the other side.

He looked around, immediately confused. Somehow, he'd made it to a fully functional hospital, its overhead lights dimmed for evening hours. He could hear the quiet rustling of people moving through the halls.

Michael's patience had worn thin. He couldn't believe none of the guys told him part of the building was still functioning. Ralph was out of his goddamn mind to buy this place.

He strolled along the hallway, wondering where the exits were. He wasn't going into a stairwell again—he'd just have to brave the storm and find his way around the building. Then he paused, realizing the storm had stopped.

A woman suddenly appeared from around the corner, startled when she saw him. She wore a hat over her clipped hair and hospital whites. "Excuse me, sir? What are you doing out of your room?"

Though highly irritated, Michael offered her a smile. "Hiya, miss. I got a little turned around. Can you show me how to get out of this place? I left a couple buddies of mine in the other rooms."

Her mouth tightened. "Patients aren't allowed to be wandering the halls at night."

"Look, lady, I ain't no patient." Michael attempted to rein in his building temper. "In fact, I'm getting a little pissed off right now. Tell me how to get out of here or you can get the hell outta my way."

"Security!" she called without skipping a beat.

Out of nowhere, Michael was bum-rushed by two men. He threw one of them off, struggling with the other as he fished for his gun. He cursed when he realized he'd left it upstairs in the broad's room. The big guy he'd thrown recovered and slammed him to the ground, pressing an arm down on his neck. Michael felt his windpipe crush as he laughed. They had no idea what they were in for.

"We're gonna need backup, Ms. Rebecca."

The woman nodded, removing a leather pouch from her apron pocket as she moved forward. In a series of quick movements, she had a needle prepared and pressed against his skin. Michael stared in disbelief as she jammed it into his arm and the best high he ever had quickly smacked him in the face.

He fought to stay conscious as the men hoisted him off the ground and onto a stretcher, tying down his limp arms and legs. He tried to make words, but they came out garbled, and he spit up on his shirt as he tried to speak.

"Take him to the basement for now," the nurse told them. "We don't want him riling up the other patients. I'll fetch Ms. Dobby."

Her blurred silhouette faded as they began rolling him down the hall to the elevator. Michael let out another garbled sound of protest as he heard them slam the gate and turn the dial, forcing the car into motion. It squeaked and moaned as it descended, and Michael faded in and out until it stopped. Even in his altered state, he could smell the stench of death immediately. It reminded him of the meat locker at the butcher's shop he used to work in as a kid.

They pushed him forward, and down another hall, this one painted so dark, he couldn't even see where the shadows ended and walls began. He looked up to see the ceiling had been covered by a long, hanging cage. Mortified, he realized it held actual patients, their sores oozing where the caustic metal bit into their flesh. Moaning, they reached down to try and grab him, their eyes shrunken so far into their heads that they looked dead.

He squeezed shut his eyes. *You're hallucinating, Mikey,* his rational mind told him. *It's the drugs, buddy. Hang in there.*

Someone slammed their fists on the cage above, forcing his eyes open. An older broad sneered down at him, her shriveled, naked body pressed into a painful pattern from the metal. Her limbs were covered in bruises, and from her left arm seeped a horrid yellow-green pus that dripped right onto his forehead. She let loose a toothless cackle as he promptly threw up.

"Ah shit, he's puking," one of the orderlies said. They picked up the pace, finally wheeling him into what looked like an old kitchen. The cold air hit Michael like a brick, stopping the vomit. He coughed, grateful.

"Should we just leave him?" one asked the other.

"That's what Lucy said." The other shrugged. "It's on her if Dobby doesn't like it."

The two reached an agreement and headed out of the room, leaving Michael with his thoughts and vodka vomit on his shoulder. He tried to ignore the smell and the hallucination of pus dripping on him when he realized whatever they'd given him had already begun to fade. He was starting to come to.

He pulled at his restraints, angry to discover they were the full-strength, hospital-grade kind they used for the real loonies. "I'm gonna kill the entire lot of these fucks," he muttered to himself. If he couldn't get himself out, either Mouse or Ralph would raise hell. He just had to be patient.

His eyesight finally adjusted to the darkness, offering a glimpse of his surroundings. The old kitchen looked like it had been out of operation for a long time; only the sink and shelves full of weird bottles remained. He searched for any means of escape when he realized with a start that someone was lying on a gurney next to him. He blinked, trying to clear his vision and his mind until it dawned on him that it was a corpse. *This ain't a kitchen at all; it's a fucking morgue.*

He pulled at his restraints harder, rocking the gurney back and forth with his weight. It shook before finally toppling over to the ground in a loud clash. He tried to use his body to scoot forward, but it was no use. He was stuck, staring at the floor in front of a giant refrigerator.

"What in the world—oh."

"What are you laughing at?"

A woman crouched down before him. It took him a minute to realize it was that damn Lisette broad.

"What are you doing? Get me out of here!" he growled.

Lisette sighed. She was dressed in similar nursing clothes as the broad who put him here, but her skirts were so long they hid her gorgeous legs. "I'm afraid I can't do that. And I definitely can't lift that gurney on my own. You'll have to wait for the orderlies."

"Well, fucking call them!" Michael sputtered. "My arm is going numb, and it smells like shit on this floor!"

"Oh, honey, I don't care about your comfort in the slightest." She stood and flipped on a light switch. Electricity buzzed and flickered, barely producing light.

Michael tried a different approach. "Look, you seem like a real class act. Can ya just go back to the wing we were in and get my friends to help? I won't hold anything against ya, I promise."

"The wing with your friends?" she snorted. "What on earth are you talking about?"

A man burst through the door. "Forgive me, my love. I'm here."

Michael stared in disbelief. It was Harold, the real estate agent. Except he was wearing an oddly fitting gray suit with a purple patterned shirt underneath, and though he could barely see, Michael swore an ugly gray wig sat on his head.

"I'm gonna ruin you, pal," he growled between clenched teeth. "I'm gonna whoop you good, then I'm gonna ruin you."

Harold chuckled nervously. "Now, now. No sense in all that. This is a wellness hospital."

"*I don't give a fuck about your hospital!*"

"He's so foul-mouthed," Lisette sniffed. "Can we gag him?"

"Oh yes, of course, dear."

Michael felt the gurney righted, blood rushing to his head just in time for Harold to shove some kind of cloth in his mouth. He let out a muffled scream even though he knew he was pointless. He was quickly running out of options. All he could do was listen.

"What is he talking about, 'his friends?'" Lisette asked.

"He's from beyond; the 1940s, to be exact. He and his friends are about to swindle the hotel from us."

Lisette stomped her foot. "So we *do* lose the hotel. You promised we wouldn't!"

"I just need more time," he said in a soothing voice, like the one a parent would use on a kid. Michael closed his eyes. Man, he missed his kids.

"You need to trust me, Lisette," Harold said.

"I'm tired, Harold," she pouted. "I'm tired of this stupid charade."

"I promise we'll hop soon. I found the perfect era for us both, and it'll let us keep the hotel infinitely."

"I'm not pretending to be a nurse again," she warned him. "You said I could do as I pleased once we were wed. This whole experiment was not in our arrangement. I do not wish to be poor or in servitude."

He took her arms. "My love, I promise I will get us out of this. No more hospitals. I will make money another way, and you will live as you should."

Michael thought about how many times he delivered the same speech to Maria. Never had he wanted to be home again so bad. *God, if you get me out of this, I'll never mess around with another broad ever again.*

A horrible scent filled his nostrils suddenly and his eyes popped open to see Harold's smile as he held a wet cloth to his nose. He knocked out easily, the combination of exhaustion and stress giving no resistance. He dreamed of Maria when she was young, the way her soft supple thighs wrapped around him. He thought of being a kid, and the church bells ringing every Sunday, letting him know Mass was almost over and it was time for Ma's pancakes.

His dreams were tossed to the side with a torrent of cold water.

"What the f—" he sputtered.

"Language or I will gag you again," a woman's voice grated at his ears. It was Lisette again, hovering over him with a pitcher of water.

"I'm sorry, I'm sorry. Please, get me out of here. I have a wife and kids—"

"It's not even medicine you know," she said as she slammed the pitcher down on the nearby table. "What he gives the patients here. It's just some recipe created by the charlatan we stole the hotel back from. That's who Harold is dressed up as in those ridiculous purple suits."

"I won't say a word, ma'am," Michael promised, hating how pathetic he sounded. How many times had guys begged him for their lives? He hated being on the other side. It just wasn't right.

"So Michael, is it?"

"Yes, ma'am," he said, trying to sound pleasant. Perhaps he could charm his way out of this situation. He wished the guys would wake up by now.

Lisette sighed, seating herself daintily on the edge of the gurney. "It's a shame we met like this. You are quite handsome. But the point is, I'm tired of Harold and his games. He has yet to deliver anything he ever promised. I am hopping by myself this time. The hotel belongs to me—she *knows* me. He doesn't hold domination over me or her." She jumped to her feet for emphasis, brushing her skirt.

"Tell me whatever you need, Ms. Listette," Michael said softly. "You are a beautiful woman. I'll help you however I can."

"I know I'm beautiful," she told him. "And I do not require the help of any man." She marched over to the refrigerator behind him and wrenched it open.

Michael struggled to see inside, but she took hold of the gurney, shoving it backward.

"Hey! Hey, what are you—"

It all happened faster than he could wrap his mind around.

The cold air from the refrigerator, the loud thud as he hit the wall. *The smell, oh God, the smell...* He thrashed around wildly, pulling at the restraints with all his might.

Lisette lingered at the doorway, gazing at him sadly. "Sorry about your wife and kids," she offered. "But they are probably better off without you."

Michael started to scream, but the air was pulled from his lungs. For in the last bit of light he was given before she closed the door, he saw the blue and bloated corpses stacked around him. His eyes clamped on the bodies of Ralph and Mouse, still tied to their gurneys, their mouths frozen in silent screams.

"Welcome to Meadowbrook," she said before she slammed the door.

There was nothing left to do but shriek as he realized he was following the path of his brothers one last time.

CHAPTER EIGHT

Helen, 1921

It was a cold winter's day when Helen had her first miscarriage. She remembered watching the snowflakes fall gently out her bathroom window as she clutched at her stomach in nothing short of agony. Remarkably, her last miscarriage also occurred in the winter, and it was the same season when Barry filed for divorce. For many, winter evoked the cozy warmth of a Christmas hearth and the laughter of family and friends. But for Helen, winter was simply a time of death.

So when she found the little boy with blue lips huddled in the kitchen pantry, only minutes after informing the girls that the winter storm was too bad this year for them to go home for the holidays, she assumed he was dead.

But his fearful eyes locked in on hers, and he let out a very alive whimper of alarm.

Children weren't allowed at Marycrest School for Girls, and even if someone had wanted to sneak a child in, there was no physical way to do it. The blizzard had ruined any chance for travel, turning the mountain the school had been built upon into a forest of endless white. Fortunately, they had enough food and supplies to last the week, but the nuns who had been sent to audit the school made it abundantly clear that no one was getting in or out for days.

Helen swallowed as fear settled in. There was simply no logical explanation for the boy's presence. She took a step closer. "What are you doing here?" she asked in a voice she hoped did not betray her fear.

The boy did not respond, continuing to stare with wide eyes.

As she moved closer, she noticed his clothes were completely soaked, hanging off a malnourished body. His pale skin was covered in cruel blossoms of green and purple bruises, and his quivering bottom lip had been split down the middle.

In a wave of maternal sympathy she always thought she'd have a chance to use but never did, she swooped down and wrapped her cardigan around his narrow shoulders. "Do you have any dry clothes with you?"

The boy shook his head.

Helen held out her hand and shivered when he reluctantly took it. His hands felt like ice.

She helped him to his feet, but he only lasted a moment before his knees buckled. Although he appeared to be eight or nine years old, he was frail enough that she could lift him up into her arms. Her mind raced as she carried him from the pantry, wondering if she should take him straight to the nuns.

What would she even say? She could picture Sister Ruth's face twisting as she tried to come up with an explanation for his presence, though she had none. Would they accuse her of deception? Relieve her of her position? And furthermore, what of the boy? Would they force him to stay in the abandoned parts of the home, as if he were a threat to the girls? She couldn't bear that. Not a child filled with bruises.

She made her decision.

Fortunately, most of the staff and nuns slept peacefully in the west wing; the girls, while most likely awake and whispering, were far above her private suite on the ground floor. The boy stirred as she carried him into her chambers, finally warming up from her body heat and the wool cardigan. When she entered her room and set him down to draw a fire, he no longer looked blue. She added an extra log to the fireplace and grabbed her kettle to make him tea.

"Have you eaten anything?" she asked him over her shoulder.

Finally, he spoke. "N-no, ma'am."

She stood and turned to look at him, hands on her hips. "Where did you come from?"

"I-I'm not sure," he looked around the room, his eyes still as wide as when she found him in the kitchen. "What is this place?"

"Meadowbrook—I mean, Marycrest School for Girls," she told him.

"I ain't never seen a school like this before," he said. "Pa never let me go to school. Gotta mind my chores." He looked down, quieting as if something bit his tongue.

"Does your Pa know you're here?"

The boy kept his head bowed, refusing to speak.

Helen began to piece things together. From the marks on his body and his physical state, he had obviously suffered abuse. He must have belonged to one of the local townsfolk that populated the nearby Meadowbrook Springs. How he managed to get here through the storm, she couldn't even imagine, but abuse can cause all sorts of desperate behavior.

She wasn't sure how she knew it, but this boy needed a mother.

She took a deep breath, steadying her nerves. "I'll need you to go into the washroom and change out of those clothes. There is a bathrobe you can use until I find you something to wear. I'm sure one of the girls has a pair of trousers; these girls come from all sorts of backgrounds." Her voice became more assertive as she spoke, slipping back into her administrative role. "I will need you to stay here and be quiet while I fetch you some supper. No one can know you are here while I consider what to do with you."

The boy looked up at her with such a mix of emotion it took her aback. "Thank you, ma'am."

"You will call me Ms. Helen. And your name is?"

"I-I'm not sure, ma'am."

Helen stared at him for a long pause. "I will call you Harold."

The teapot squealed.

After she'd gotten him to take a few sips of tea and showed him how to use the bathtub, she pulled on her housecoat and slipped away. Confident she would be able to move around undetected, she set her lamp down and turned on the kitchen stove.

She sighed, her mind a mess of thoughts.

Originally hired by the progressive Higglebottoms, she and several other women had been recruited for a brand new initiative to provide quality, college-level education to girls. Helen was the perfect candidate—a recent divorcee with no family in desperate need of her own money. The thought of providing an education to young women thrilled her as well; she'd been an avid reader since she was a child, and though she ended up a housewife, she finally had a chance to put her mind to use.

She could still recall the thrill she felt as the train wove them through acres of orange and yellow trees to bring them into town. The air had smelled—had tasted—of new adventures and possibilities. The gorgeous hotel-turned-school had taken her breath away, and she roamed its halls with an almost girlish excitement, mirroring the thrill from the actual girls who soon filled the halls with exuberant clatter.

But Helen and her fellow teachers tried their best, and though they succeeded for a glorious two years, wealthy families willing to send their daughter into the mountains to boarding school rather than local finishing schools proved few and far between. It cost quite a bit to maintain the school and its staff, and money was running out. Forced to pivot, the Higglebottoms discovered the families who were willing to send their daughters away were those with wayward, often pregnant, girls. Helen was not prepared for what would follow; as soon as they accepted these girls, the ones from wealthier families fled. Half of the "wayward girls" required medical care she and the other teachers struggled to provide—one even murdered her own newborn in the bathtub. They tried their best, but over time, Helen was the only teacher left standing. While she stepped firmly into her new role as House Mother, she knew things could not keep as they were.

Her suspicions were confirmed when a bus full of nuns appeared at the front steps of Meadowbrook School for Girls. The Higglebottoms, desperate for help and funding, had decided to petition the Church.

Helen had only received a letter in warning:

Dearest Helen,

Please forgive us for the late correspondence. The Sisters of Marycrest will be auditing our school to give a final report back to the Diocese in the hopes that they will provide us with the proper funding to keep our school in operation. We appreciate your cooperation in this matter and hope to bring you good news.

Warmest regards,
H. & L. Higglebottom

Within two months, the Sisters of Marycrest had rewritten Helen's entire lesson plan, marked 'unnecessary' books in the library for destruction, and affixed crucifixes to the walls of every dorm room. They cleaned out the old garden chapel and set aside time for daily devotionals. In a whirlwind, Helen's dream of watching educated women soar had quickly been dashed to the ground.

She sighed, checking to see if the stove had been lit and putting on a pot of leftover soup. She fetched a few crackers and a carton of milk, then put it all on a tray with a bowl, which she filled with warm chicken noodle soup. Then she headed upstairs, her feet padding quietly along the wood floor.

When she entered her bedroom, the boy was fast asleep on her bed, draped loosely with one of her blankets. She set the tray down on her bedside table and moved to cover him with another one when she noticed long scars crawling up his bony back, like the scars from a whip. Tears caught in her throat, and she covered him with a warmer blanket. He looked so peaceful as he slept, like he was finally safe.

She tucked a lock of brown hair behind his ear. "Welcome to Meadowbrook, Harry," she whispered.

It was the following winter when Harry told her he needed to leave.

She'd walked in to see the parlor covered with books. It wasn't an atypical scene; Harry read and digested information unlike anything she had ever seen before, and he often had piles of books at a time. Long were the nights that he kept her up with his chatter; in fact, he'd rescued most of the books the nuns deemed unsuitable for reading, keeping them carefully hidden in what was left of the east wing. But today, he had a look on his face unlike any she had seen before. It was excitement, pure and unbridled.

Helen, however, did not share his enthusiasm. "What do you mean you're going to leave?" Harold often disappeared for long hours, even days, exploring the grounds. As much as it pained her, Helen understood it was part of his curious nature. She couldn't keep him contained in her room forever; it was cruel.

"It won't be for too long. Longer than normal, but still."

He hopped to his feet, and she couldn't help but swell with pride at his appearance. Over the past year of being mothered properly, he'd grown into quite the strapping young boy. The girls of Marycrest eventually found out about her secret. They all spoiled him: extra cakes at bedtime, stories in the dorm. One of them even managed to get him a pair of glasses so he could read.

"I have it timed just right, so you'll barely even miss me," he promised.

She didn't bother to ask what he meant. "Harold, if the Sisters find you coming or going—"

"They won't. Besides, they won't be here too much longer anyway."

Helen frowned. "What do you mean?"

"I overheard them talking. The Church is not going to fund Marycrest. They want to set up an operation closer to town."

Helen's stomach sank. "What are we going to do?"

"Relax," he soothed. "That's why I have to go. I have a plan."

Helen couldn't help the smile that poked through her frustration. She knew he had a plan. He always did. There was something different about Harold, the way his brain solved puzzles, the way he knew the answers to everything you could imagine. She'd already wondered how she could get him to a proper school. The best school.

He looked up at her with earnest eyes, taking her hands in his. "My ma died when I was little, and you're the only true mother I've ever known. I will come back, I promise."

Helen felt her eyes well up with tears, too touched to speak. She knew what he told her was in earnest; it had only been a year, and she'd grown attached to him, too. They all did; every girl kept his secret, whether it was Lucy sneaking him on the grounds for hikes or Bethany using him as her study buddy. He belonged here; no one had any doubt.

"Be safe, then, Harry."

He nodded. "I plan to go tonight during your meeting with the Sisters." Before she could ask, he explained, "I overheard them saying they were going to schedule a meeting with you."

There was a knock at the front door of her suite.

Harold gave her a swift kiss on the cheek and ducked into their bedroom closet.

"Who is it?" Helen called.

"It's Lucy, ma'am."

Helen opened the door to a girl with long, mousy brown hair and big gray eyes. Her uniform hung too large around her tiny frame. "Sister Rose sent me. She needs to speak with you immediately." She leaned in to whisper. "I can watch Harold for you."

Helen surveyed the hall. "That would be wonderful, Lucy, thank you."

The girl nodded and slipped in. Helen closed and locked the door behind her. As she walked down the hall to the main lobby, her stomach squeezed. She could almost smell the thick, nauseating incense that pervaded every pore of the nun's wing. She hated it; hundreds of crucifixes lined the walls as if implying she and the girls were demons who needed warding off. Where the sight of crosses might bring some peace, they reminded Helen of death. Painful suffering and needless death.

She shivered as she navigated to the west wing lobby toward Sister Rose's office, trying to breathe through the nauseating aromas that had reached a suffocating level.

Her secretary nodded Helen through.

Sister Rose was expecting her, standing straight up behind her desk with her hands tucked into her habit. "Please sit down, Helen."

Sister Rose insisted upon wearing a full habit at all times, her entire body swallowed by black fabric except for her pinched, wrinkled face and beady eyes. Helen would never let herself turn into such an insufferable spinster.

"We have some unfortunate news," Sister Rose said as Helen settled into an uncomfortable metal chair. "The Bishop has decided against setting up here. He believes that the families we service would benefit from a closer location. We plan to leave tomorrow before the snowstorm. I believe your employer will be contacting you soon, but we wanted to let you know ahead of time so there would be no cause for concern."

Helen's heart soared at the thought of a nunless school. "I appreciate you letting me know, Sister Rose. Thank you."

"You've done wonderful work with these girls, Helen." The nun smoothed her skirts and sat. "I know the Lord has a special place in his Kingdom for you."

Helen flinched. "Thank you."

She began shuffling papers on her desk, and Helen prepared to leave.

"We will also be taking the girls with us," she added without looking up.

"Wh-whatever do you mean—"

"The six girls you have left in your ward are going to come with us to our new in-town Marycrest facility."

"Y-you can't do that," Helen sputtered. "These girls are under my care."

Sister Rose handed her a file. "Their families have all given their blessings. The care of the girls will be transferred over to the Diocese. I know this all comes as a bit of a shock for you, but we promise to offer them the same care as you have these past months."

Helen's head spun, but she managed to nod politely and thank her.

"You're dismissed, Ms. Helen."

The walk back to the east dormitory felt like a walk to her death. What would she tell them? What would she tell Lucy or Bethany? ...What would she tell Harold?

She made it to her chambers and threw open the door. "Harry? Lucy?" The echo exacerbated the shrillness in her voice.

They were nowhere to be found, but she was glad for it. The tears were coming now, and she didn't want anyone to see it. She collapsed onto her bed, heaving for breath. It had been so long since she cried, it felt like the dam of a great river had crumbled.

The next morning, her pillow was still damp when she woke.

Her head throbbing, she lifted herself off the bed to look around. "Harry?"

Then she remembered what he'd said: he planned to leave during their meeting. Despair clutched her heart, but she had no tears left. She needed to be strong for the girls—the girls. She hadn't had a chance to tell them.

She flew to her washroom to splash water on her face and

smooth her clothing, hoping no one would notice she had slept in her blouse and skirt. Then she raced to the lobby as fast as she could.

Cold air from the outside smacked her as she rounded the corner, a few preliminary snowflakes trickling in the open front door.

The Sisters of Marycrest stood in a cluster amongst piles of luggage, long black cloaks over their habits. The girls huddled together in their coats, some tearful as they watched attendants from the train station take their belongings to the cars parked outside.

Before Helen could speak, Sister Rose's angry expression blocked her view. "Where is Lucille Scott?"

Helen thought of Harry, wondering if Lucy had followed him on his travels. "If you cannot find her, then she is obviously a runaway," Helen replied coldly. "As of today, she is officially under your care, not mine. I suggest you contact the local authorities."

Sister Rose let out a sound of angry exasperation as another nun slipped beside her. "We cannot prolong the departure, Sister Rose. The gentlemen said the snow will be here soon. We have to board the train."

Sister Rose shot her look back at Helen. "I know she is here, somewhere. I just don't know if this is a stunt orchestrated by you or her."

"Well, this is certainly a far cry from 'the Lord has a special spot for me in Heaven,'" Helen remarked.

"You will contact us immediately when you find her, or I will tell the authorities that you have kidnapped one of our wards."

Helen nodded, though she was unfazed. All her sorrow had been released in tears, and her resolve had been restored.

Sister Rose stepped aside, and Helen went to the girls. "Forgive me for not saying anything. I found out last night."

Madeline, a gentle soul with an addled mind, wrapped her arms around her. "Why can't you come with us?"

"I'm quite sure the church would not have me," she said, as Bethany followed suit with another embrace.

"You will visit though?"

"Of course, I will," Helen lied. She knew the Sisters of Marycrest wouldn't let a divorced apostate like Helen anywhere near any of them again.

"Girls," Sister Rose called.

The nuns were filling out into the gentle snow, not unlike the pictures Helen had seen of penguins waddling. She finished up her farewells, trying not to laugh at the absurdity of it all. Then she took a step back, watching as each girl climbed into the bus behind them.

Sister Rose gave her one last cold appraisal. "Good afternoon, Ms. Helen. Be sure to call us immediately when you find Lucille. We will send a car up to fetch her as soon as the snow stops."

Helen nodded and the dreadful nun headed down the front steps and into her car. Helen waved to the van holding the girls as they headed down the long driveway, struck by the conflicting emotions of regret and relief as they finally disappeared around the bend.

They were gone.

Helen headed back into the hotel, locking the front doors behind her. Silence greeted her. She realized that, for the first time, she was completely alone.

There were no servants, no wait staff, no cook, no cleaners, no one. Just her and an old, cavernous hotel. She took a deep breath, realizing she was shaking. She just had to get through the next few days until Harry came back. And hopefully, she'd hear from the Higgenbottoms soon.

She debated lighting the main fireplace in the center of the room, knowing its massive size and girth did wonders to kill the winter chill, but she didn't want to chance a wayward fire. Nor did she want to spend her time in an empty, echoing shell as the winter storm closed in. She wanted to feel cozy. Perhaps now she would have a chance to read.

She took her leave of the lobby and retreated to her chambers. Taking another steadying breath, she opened the curtains to a flurry of white. Then she stoked the fire in her fireplace, made her bed, and drew herself a hot bath.

The rest of the day was a welcome reprieve after years of tending to children. Helen found solace in the fact that she had no one around to appease. The Higgenbottoms had always been good to her; even if she had to leave Meadowbrook, she knew they'd help her find additional lodging. She had enough money saved to afford it; the problem was where would she go? Making sure Harry got the proper education was the most important thing, but it was hard to find landlords who would rent to a single woman, let alone one with a child. Still, that was a problem for another day. Today was about peace.

By the time the sun set, the storm had reached its full peak. As Helen closed the curtains, she heard the hotel moan against the snowy squalls. She'd long grown used to the sound of the building settling, but heavy winds against a towering mountaintop hotel never ceased to make her wary.

Her stomach growled, and she realized that, although she'd consumed several cups of tea, she hadn't eaten. She found her housecoat and slippers and headed back to the dark, ominous lobby. Although her footsteps were padded, they echoed in the quiet, and she began to hum quietly to herself.

The lights flickered as she crossed the dining hall, and a horrifying thought struck through her calm—what if the power went out? She picked up her pace to the kitchen, relieved when she found a few gas lamps on a corner shelf. She set them out to easily find later and made sure to light one before she retrieved yesterday's stew from the ice box. She warmed it up on the stove, suddenly missing Harry as she prepared a tray for only one. Then she grabbed her gaslamp and headed back to her room.

It was an hour later when her worry came true.

But Helen chose to smile, grateful she'd grabbed the lamp. She also kept several candles in her cabinet and she set to work bathing her room in a pleasant glow. She'd grabbed her book and prepared one last cup of tea before bed when she heard the noise. She paused, harkening her ears.

It was as if someone was moving around in the girls' dorm directly above her. She grew excited for a moment, thinking it was Harry. Then she remembered—Lucy. Perhaps Lucy hadn't gone along with Harold after all.

She sighed and put the tea kettle back. She couldn't imagine how terrified Lucy must feel hiding up there with no lights. She stuffed a few candles in her housecoat pockets and withdrew into the hallway. "Lucy?" she called.

Nothing but wind responded.

Unable to use the elevator, and knowing the stairwell would be far too dark and harrowing to navigate in lamplight, Helen had no choice but to use the main lobby stairs.

The lobby itself was unsettlingly dark without any lighting, and Helen was forced to squint just to see a few feet in front of her. She located the fireplace with its whitewashed stones, a lighthouse in a sea of shadows. From there, she found the stairwell, which she took gingerly, making sure she had her footing each time before she climbed.

"Lucy?" she called softly when she reached the second floor.

She was hit with a pang of sorrow seeing the dorm so empty. Just yesterday, it had been filled with the warmth of whispering girls. They all had their demons, but Helen knew that deep down, they were good. One couldn't help how one was raised—even rich families had their fair share of dark secrets—but she had faith in them all. She could only hope the nuns would treat them the same.

"Lucy?"

Nothing.

Helen wondered if she'd heard anything at all. Perhaps it was a rat, or a pile of snow falling from a tree branch. The wind whistled outside, and suddenly Helen wanted to be back, safe and cozy, in her room.

Then she heard it again—footsteps. It was coming from the third floor, not the second.

"Dammit, Lucy."

The third and fourth floors had been deemed off-limits for the girls; the owner responsible for rebuilding it after the fire hadn't finished the renovations before it was sold. Helen hadn't even visited the upper floors; the Higglebottoms hadn't given her any reason to question their rules. As frustrated as she was, Helen had to admit the third floor would be the perfect place for a runaway; even the nuns dared not explore.

Helen lifted her skirt high enough to climb over the boards that created a shoddy blockade to the third floor. The only window at the far end of the hall had been boarded up, making the third floor so dark that she could see no farther than what the lamp's halo revealed. Her heart rate started to climb as she started to convince herself why going forward was not a good idea. What if there were upturned nails or broken glass that would pierce her house shoes? What if the floor was damaged and she fell through?

A muffled voice came from one of the rooms.

"Hello, Lucy? Lucy, it's Ms. Helen. It's safe to come out."

Growing frustrated by the lack of response, Helen burst through one of the doors. Then another. Then another. Finally, she made it to the door at the end of the hall. Her teeth chattered, the boarded window unable to keep out the winter chill. She pushed it open and revealed none other than Lucy.

"Ms. Helen?" She looked confused. "It's not time for you yet."

"What on earth are you talking about, young lady? You made me worried to death—I've been calling for you."

"I–I just got here. Come inside the door, Ms. Helen. You shouldn't be in the hall right now." Lucy grabbed her arm.

Helen caught her eye, and realized with a start that Lucy looked different than yesterday. Older, even. She wasn't wearing her uniform either, instead in a form-fitting skirt and cardigan in a style unlike anything Helen had ever seen.

"Mother? Mother, I'm here."

Helen pulled away from her. "Harry?"

"Helen, no, don't go out there—" Lucy tried desperately to grab her arm, but it was too late.

Helen saw Harry's thin frame down the hall, his pale skin glowing in the shadows.

She grinned, happy he made it back so quickly. She walked forward to greet him, eager to feel his little hands in hers, when suddenly, a dark, billowing shadow appeared behind him.

Helen had no time to react. In a moment too fast to properly register a horrified scream, two shadowy arms burst forward, wrapping around Harry's neck. She dropped her lamp, and the fire that blew up around her cast light on the worst things a mother could see—her son's terrified face as the shadowy arms and hands became corporeal and twisted, snapping his neck like a twig.

She fell to her knees as his limp body crumbled to the ground, her gut-wrenching screams released. They flooded the foyer as the flames threatened to do the same.

"P.J., the boards—hurry!"

Helen lost all sense of reality as things floated before her. It was as if she'd left her body, the frantic figures around her just moving pictures on the screen. She watched the killer shadow—now an actual man—walk forward and pry the boards from the window. She watched the flames lick her sweet son's body as Lucy flew from the room.

"Lucy, get her out of here!"

"What about the body?"

She watched another man, stout and bespectacled, race through the fire to assist the black man. Finally, the bitter wind and snow were released, halting the fire's spread. Helen couldn't see Harry anymore through the flames, and in a burst of hysteria, she scrambled toward him. A pair of strong arms grabbed her then, and she heard a familiar voice in her ear.

"Mom, it's me. Mom, it's me. It's Harold." He said it again and again as she fought him, unable to comprehend what he was telling her, the vision of her dying son playing cruelly on repeat before her eyes.

"Mom, I had to kill him because he's me. I am Harold, all grown up."

"W-what?" Helen struggled to understand, the smoke from the slowly extinguishing fire choking her. She felt dizzy, the sounds of cracking wood and wild wind in her ears. Then she collapsed, unable to comprehend anymore; the last thing she saw was a man holding her, flames in his eyes.

———

Helen woke screaming.

"Shhh, it's okay, Ms. Helen," Lucy soothed.

Helen struggled to make sense of her world. She was in her room, safe in bed, near a roaring fire. It was still snowing, but sunlight poked through the flakes to fill her bedroom. Lucy, an older version of the Lucy she knew, sat at her bedside with a glass of water. From the lines on her face, she looked as if she'd aged twenty years.

Helen grabbed the water with shaking hands.

"The fire," she sputtered.

"Harold and P.J. put it out. You're safe now."

The blood drained from Helen's face. "Harold...*Harry...*"

"Helen, listen to me. I don't want you to faint again. This is very shocking, but Harold is alive, he's just older now. He's a full-grown man. We want to explain everything to you, but you have to calm down, okay?"

Helen took a deep breath and another sip of water. "Please let me see Harry."

The door opened, and in walked her son. She knew it was him; a mother always knows her child. But he was older, as Lucy said; in fact, he looked to be about thirty years of age. Still wearing his pop-bottle glasses, but they had thick, speckled rims. His hair was thicker and longer, and he wore a shirt with a high collar and blue jeans.

"Harry?" she whimpered.

"Hi, Mom." He swooped down and hugged her, and although the situation was impossible, she somehow knew everything would be okay. As long as he was with her.

She pulled away, tears spilling down her cheeks. "Where did you go? How did you grow up so fast?"

He took her hands, surprising her with their warmth. "I've figured out how to travel back and forth through time."

"Harry, that sounds like madness."

"It's true," Lucy echoed from across the room.

Harold pulled her attention back to him. "Mom, this place has certain properties, unlike anything anyone has ever seen. I have made it my life's work to study it. I believe Meadowbrook serves as a liminal space created from the magic of the nearby springs. I believe that is how I first came to be here, with you. Before I left, I filled my time mapping out all of the portals and have spent the last thirty jumping back and forth throughout time. Well, thirty for me. I only aged twenty."

Helen studied his face, shocked by the earnestness in his eyes. "B-but it's only been a day since you left."

Harold grinned. "I'm getting very good at what I do, Mom. You'd have been so proud of me."

Helen's heart sank as realization hit her. "I didn't get to raise you."

"Of course you did," he said, squeezing her hands. "And you will now. I've learned everything there is to know about this hotel and the different timelines, and I'm taking you with me."

"Timelines?"

"Yes, each timeline has a set of events that I must be wary of as I travel. That's why I had P.J. kill my younger self—if you meet yourself at any point, one of you will die. Young Me had to go so I could reach you."

Helen's head started to hurt.

"This is probably too much for her," Lucy said.

"No." Helen took another sip of water. "I want to understand."

Harold grinned again, the same boyish smile she remembered from his youth. *Had it only been two days?*

"Who is P.J.?"

Harold looked at Lucy, who immediately moved to fetch him.

"I met P.J. during my travels," Harold explained, "when we were boys. We've been traveling together ever since. He is my dearest friend."

Lucy returned, followed by the tall black man Helen had seen earlier. In the light, he didn't look as terrifying, but Helen couldn't get the image of him murdering her son out of her mind. So she focused on his eyes, a soft brown that betrayed his gentleness beyond his stature.

Harold made a few gestures with his hands, and P. J. responded similarly. Helen realized the man was deaf.

"He says he's sorry you had to see all that," Harold told her.

"Tell him it's okay," Helen said softly.

"He can read your lips. Though it's much easier to sign. It made teaching him everything I learned at University a breeze."

Helen let out a sound of happiness. "You went to school?"

Harold beamed. "I did. I became a lawyer. I had to so I could purchase the hotel—"

"Wait, you bought Meadowbrook? From the Higglebottoms?"

"Well, not exactly. That's why we're here. To collect you and resume renovations on the hotel. I have great plans." His eyes sparkled.

"But Harry, how will you get the money?"

"That's the thing, Mom. I've thought of everything. Lucy and I *are* the Higglebottoms. We have a special account where I store all the money I acquire during my travels."

Lucy perked up from where she sat in the corner. "Harold inherited the hotel when he marr—"

Harold stood to silence her. "I want to focus on the present. I want to focus on you and I, darling."

Helen let out another incredulous sound. "Have you married?"

Harold beamed, pulling Lucy into the crook of his arm. "We have. Somewhere between 1947 and 1950."

Lucy laughed.

Helen took another sip of water. "How do you keep track of it all?"

Harold shrugged. "You know me. I always have a plan."

As overwhelmed as she was, Helen couldn't help but smile. "Yes, you do."

Harold crouched back down to her side. "This is my hotel. It has picked me, of all the people in this world, to be its caretaker. I have plans to make this timeline an oasis for tired souls. A place where we can live, forever."

"Harry," Lucy said softly. "This is a lot. Let's talk again over dinner. You'd like that, right, Ms. Helen? A proper dinner with a proper staff?"

"Staff?"

"Yes, they're already on their way. I have connections on the outside for when we time-hop, and they've already sent over the cooks and waitstaff."

"Oh, Harry. This is all happening so fast."

"It will be okay, Mom. You have to trust me."

Helen looked up into her sweet Harry's eyes, sitting in the face of a full-grown man. "Is this really going to work, Harold?" she whispered.

"Oh yes, Mother. It will."

CHAPTER NINE
Percy, 1905-1910

The scent of blood soured his nostrils as he hid in the tiny closet, trying to quiet his thumping heart. He felt the vibration of footsteps continue outside as the man searched for him. Percy didn't want to think about what he would do if he found him. He was in a different time—a time he'd been warned would bring him danger. He squeezed his eyes shut, trying to ignore the blood on his hands, thinking instead of Mama and the gentle rumble of her chest as she sang to soothe him.

"This hotel is different, PJ," she'd mouth to him when he was a child. He always read her lips; she never had to sign. "Don't stray too far, no matter how curious you get. It will take you from me."

He always thought it was strange she warned him like that. He never even considered leaving her side, even when she took the new job at the hospital. Mama was sharp as hell and had no issue convincing the pinched-faced lady she was an actual nurse. She did this by pretending she wasn't smart.

"I left my paperwork when I ran away from my husband," she told her, clutching Percy's hand with forced tears. "Please, ma'am. I can't let him know where I'm at."

The old white woman sighed. "Well, your application is already complete, and you've tested well in all areas. I suppose you can start as a nursing assistant until you get your paperwork in."

"Thank you so much, ma'am."

The woman looked straight at Percy. "Can he understand me?"

"He can read lips and sign. P.J. won't be too much trouble at all. He's content with his books and puzzles."

The woman sighed again. "Alright, Miss June. Welcome to Meadowbrook Psychiatric Hospital. You can start tomorrow."

"I hate that you talk about Dad like that," Percy signed to her after they returned home to the chapel. They'd been hiding out there since the last jump after Mama figured out they'd turned the hotel into some kind of hospital. They only jumped twice since Percy was born, and she wanted to make sure this time was safe.

Mama had stopped folding laundry to study his face with her kind but stern brown eyes. "I know, P.J., but we gotta do what we gotta do in each world we find ourselves in. Let me get us settled into the hospital. Then we can try to figure out how to find your daddy. Okay?"

Percy nodded, for he trusted her. He had no reason not to until the day he met Mei.

The old white hospital lady, Mrs. Bartleby, gave them a nice little suite in the employee wing of the building. Percy was glad to get out of that old chapel, but spending hours alone in their set of rooms got old fast. Mama always brought him new books and toys, but that only kept him occupied for so long. Eventually, it was time to explore.

It had been a warm summer morning, and he'd been reading in the common room. A few nurses waltzed in, oblivious to his presence. Most of them treated him that way by default; he was quiet and he couldn't hear, so they thought nothing of gossiping in front of him. Little did they know Percy had perfected the art of reading their lips above his open chapter book.

"Did you hear?" One of the nurses started. "Someone put a bid on the other half of the hotel."

"The burned wing? They can't be serious. That would take years to repair."

"Apparently not that long. Besides, the lobby is still perfectly renovated. It's just sitting there waiting."

One of the nurses shook her head. "No one wants to stay at a hotel that's attached to a loony bin. It's a terrible idea."

"Well, you know these businessmen and their awful ideas. As long as I get my paycheck, I don't pay it no mind."

They moved away to where Percy could no longer see them, but his interest peaked regardless. He knew part of the hotel was boarded up and off-limits, but he had no idea it was all fixed up. Curiosity gripped him, and he devised a plan.

Meadowbrook's patients were most active right before dinner, and he knew all he had to do was walk calmly through the chaos. Mama would be too busy cooking in the kitchen to see him either. She worked well into the evening—they had most of the nurses on double shifts—and wouldn't be home until he was half-asleep anyway. In the back of his mind, he knew Mama would disapprove of his little adventure, but he truly believed there was no harm in it. He'd be home and in bed before she even knew he was gone. The only thing he needed was the key.

He headed to his room to pack a bag. He smashed in a notebook to record his journey, a sketch pad, a water bottle, an apple, and a pack of crackers. Then he was out, excitement tickling his belly.

As planned, no one paid him any mind.

The patients left in the lobby were heavily sedated. Percy felt bad for them, but Mama insisted it was for their own good. A lot of them had brain sickness so bad that they would hurt themselves and others. Still, it never felt right to him to keep humans that way.

He walked right into the empty nurse's station and looked around. On the wall were several clearly labeled spare room keys, but he couldn't find one for the separating wall. He let out a sigh of frustration before his eyes found the file cabinet. Along the side, sure enough, was a brand new key labeled 'L'. That had to be it. He snatched the key and hurried down the hallway to the newly built separating wall. He found the door and pushed the key into it. Remarkably, it worked.

As soon as he entered the lobby, he felt uneasy. It had been beautifully renovated to look like a hotel from another time, then abandoned, a layer of dust built up on the pretty gold fixtures and dark wood furniture. Percy tried to explain once to Mama how he felt the energy of things, but it was hard to put into words. He felt it now, radiating off the shadowy stairwell and clinging to the rugs. This part of the hotel breathed stories, but Percy knew only a few could *hear* them.

Sun squeezed through boarded-up windows and doors, leaving zigzag patterns along Percy's skin as he shuffled along the hall. At the center of the room was a massive whitewashed fireplace with a strange owl sculpture at the center. It almost looked like a gargoyle from where he stood, and for a moment, Percy imagined what it would be like to see the hotel in full operation.

Then he saw her.

He let out a surprised sound and jumped back.

The girl said nothing. She wore a simple medical gown underneath a waterfall of black hair. She stared at him with somber eyes.

Unsure what to do, Percy waved.

The girl waved back.

Percy tried to form words. Throughout his life, people's eyes mocked him for his vocalizations, so he normally kept quiet. "Can you talk?"

The girl shook her head.

"I can't hear." He showed her the sign for 'deaf.' "Can you sign?"

"No. Little," she tried to sign.

Percy frowned. This would be more difficult than he thought. "You a patient here?"

She nodded sadly.

"You shouldn't be here. I can take you back—"

She shook her head furiously.

Percy was confused until he remembered his bag. He pulled out the notepad and handed it to her. She seemed worried, but he watched her awkwardly draw her letters. NO ENGLISH. NO WORDS.

"You can understand me, but you can't spell?"

She nodded.

"Okay. You don't want to go back to the hospital?"

She shook her head again, then gestured for him to follow.

"Isn't that part of the hotel burned up?"

But she was already heading that way.

Percy folded and stuck the notebook in his pocket, and hurried to catch up. He spotted the entrance to a cavernous ballroom out of the corner of his eye, as well as a gold, inoperable elevator. An acrid, unpleasant smell filled his nostrils as he headed deeper into the east wing and soon, he saw the aftermath of fire.

The nurses were right; there was no way cleaning this part of the hotel up would be an easy task. Parts of the ceiling had long caved in, leaving the floor a mess of boards and shattered glass. Mushrooms and plant growth reclaimed most of the structure. A cool breeze whistled in through the open walls.

Percy saw no sign of the girl. "Hello?" he called.

He thought of Mama's warnings then. *"Don't stray too far, no matter how curious you get. It will take you from me."*

He decided to turn around when suddenly he saw the girl's head pop around the corner. Relieved, he walked over to greet her where she stood in the doorway. She moved to the side, and Percy entered, shocked to see the room was fully intact. It had a similar look to the lobby, with brand-new fancy furniture and light fixtures, as if the entire place had been spared from the fire.

He felt someone touch his arm and he jumped back in alarm.

Standing before him was a slender white lady wearing a fancy blue dress that ballooned out at her hips. "Can you hear me?"

Percy tried to gather his wits as Mei shyly peered from around the woman.

"It's okay, Percy," the woman said with a smile. "We are all friends here. Come, sit."

"How do you know my name?"

Remarkably, the woman signed back to him. "I know your father."

Percy struggled to catch his breath. His father? He didn't know what was going on, but he couldn't run away. Not now. He was far too curious.

"I have been learning to sign with Mei," the woman continued. "My name is Ms. Lisette and I am one of the owners of Meadowbrook. Please do sit, dear. You look like you're going to faint."

Percy could do nothing but fall into one of the upholstered chairs.

Ms. Lisette settled down across from him on the loveseat, but Mei remained standing upright, a few feet away from them near the door. He couldn't read her expression.

"Delby? Can you please bring us some tea?" Lisette called over her shoulder. Then she turned back to Percy, studying him with her light eyes. "My, you look just like him."

"You know my daddy?"

"Oh yes," she said. "He's been looking for you for a long time. Your mother has tried to keep you sequestered in specific periods, as she should. But we are all moving, whether we like it or not. My husband refuses to let us stay put."

Percy found himself at a loss for words. A part of him knew Daddy was out looking for him and Mama. But she'd refused to believe it.

A man entered the room wearing a black and white suit and carrying a silver tray. He set it down on the table in front of him.

"Thank you, Delby," Lisette said. "Can you bring our guest some snacks as well?"

"I-I brought my own, thank you," Percy signed.

"Very well." Lisette used a thin silver utensil to grab two sugar cubes from a bowl and drop them into a cup. Then she lifted the tea kettle, steam drifting around her ears.

Percy took a deep breath. "Is my daddy here?"

"Yes and no. However, I can tell you where to find him. But I will need a favor from you in return.

"What is it?"

Lisette stirred her tea with a small silver spoon. "Do you know how I found Mei? She was starving and cold, trapped inside the passageways Harold built when he renovated the hotel. She came from a time when they locked up and sedated human beings simply for being different. Mei is of sound mind; she is simply mute. Her native language is not like ours, which makes it even more difficult to communicate. But instead of attempting to understand this, they believed her to be unruly and mad. So they kept her caged, like an animal. And do you know the man who created the hospital that could do such a thing? My deplorable husband, that's who."

Percy looked at Mei, who remained quiet in the shadows.

"He's also responsible for separating your mother and father. And numerous other egregious behaviors. He keeps us all trapped here, and he must be stopped."

Percy sorted through her words. One man had destroyed his family?

Lisette took a sip of her tea. "Mei will guide you to the time when you can reunite with your father. During that time period, you will meet a little boy named Harold. He will have no idea about his power yet. I will need you to kill him."

"I can't kill nobody!"

Lisette seemed amused. "What if I told you I met you when you were an adult? That I have been time-hopping for decades? You have killed men, PJ. Rest assured, you have never been shy there."

Percy felt as if he might cry at any moment. He felt Mei come up beside him and gently put a hand on his shoulder.

"There is no other way," Lisette said gently. "You simply have to take him to the east wing pool and push him in. We just put it in last summer. Harold cannot swim. He'll sink to the ground like a rock—as he should have decades ago. Then all of our problems are over. There will be no more random time-hopping—no more fear that our world will suddenly shift and we'll lose everything. Things will be as they should be. We will all be free."

Percy stared at the woman before him, at her icy eyes and manic smile, and realized she was crazy. He wanted to run back to Mama —she'd know exactly how to handle her. But he also wanted to find Daddy, and this might be his only chance. There was a reason he found Mei and a reason she brought him here. He closed his eyes, wondering what Mama would do. Then it hit him—she would lie.

"Okay, I will do it," Percy told Lisette. "But I need to get back home to Mama after."

Lisette beamed. "Absolutely. You take care of our Harold problem, and Mei will guide you back to your time. With Harold's death, I will become the hotel's sole mistress. You have my word. Your family will be united once more."

Percy nodded.

"Mei, show Percy to the tunnels."

The muffled sounds of shouting reached Percy's ears, interrupting his memories of what brought him there. He was back in the present time, and other men had come to join the search for him. He wished with every cell in his body that he hadn't agreed to come here. He never should have listened to that crazy woman; he had no idea where Mei was or how he was going to get back. And that's if the angry white men didn't kill him first. All he could hope for now was that Mei had gotten away. He accepted whatever happened to him was his own fault. He should have just listened to Mama.

A pair of footsteps, much lighter this time, approached the closet door. Percy took a deep breath and clamped his eyes closed. This was it. He was done for. All he could do now was pray it would be over quick.

The door creaked open, but surprisingly, nothing grabbed him. He popped open one eye, then both when he saw what the opened door revealed. Standing before him was a young boy in glasses, frantically gesturing for him to follow. "Come with me right now, and don't say a word!"

Percy struggled to make sense of what was happening.

"Come on!"

Percy jumped up, and the boy pulled him into the bathroom, where he turned on the faucet over a tub. He watched the boy's mouth as he tried frantically to explain. "The only way to get you outta this room is through the water in the tub. I know it sounds crazy, but you gotta trust me—they are searching for you bad. They know you witnessed him kill that Black man."

Percy nodded, realizing the boy meant a jump. He'd never heard of going through water before, but he was running out of options. He looked out the window, searching for any sight of Mei.

"Come on, we have to do this now!"

Percy gingerly climbed into the tub, surprised when the boy pushed his head under. He fought him for a minute—though they were the same age, Percy was much bigger and he knew he could overpower him—but something inside him knew it was the only way. Finally, he relented, closing his eyes and picturing Mama's face. Her soft amber eyes. The way her hair sprang up on warm days. Maybe if he was lucky, he'd see her again...

Percy burst to the top of some watery surface, gasping for air. Unable to swim, he struggled to keep from sinking until two small arms reached down to pull him up. The taste of the water was rancid, and he quickly realized he was in a pond. His legs kicked in panic, fortunately working to help the boy pull them both to the edge. Percy pulled himself the rest of the way and collapsed onto the grassy bank. Then he retched, continuing to spit in disgust until he couldn't spit anymore.

Then, both boys lay still, flat on their backs, panting in the grass. White fluffy clouds drifted overhead, calming them both.

Finally, Percy felt a vibration come from the boy, letting him know he was talking. Percy sat up and turned to face him. "I'm deaf," he mouthed as touched his lips, then his ear.

The boy also sat up, his blue eyes wide. "Can you read lips?"

Percy nodded.

"Can you sign?" the boy asked with his hands.

Percy blinked, taken aback.

"There was an old sign language book left behind at the hotel," the boy spelled with his fingers. "I like to learn things, so I taught myself. I taught myself Spanish and French too."

Percy couldn't believe his luck. "Nice to meet you. My name is Percy."

"Hi, Percy. I'm Harold."

Every hair on Percy's skin rose. He couldn't believe it. He'd found the infamous Harold.

"You okay, Percy?"

Percy snapped out of it. "Uh yes. I didn't know you could jump through water."

"Time-hop, you mean? Oh, yes. Water is the easiest way. Water, stairwells, elevators, death…" He fished through his pockets to pull out his glasses, which he shook off before pushing onto his squat nose. He looked around. "I know where we are."

Percy followed his gaze. The hotel spires peeked out from behind a distant treeline, not more than a mile away; it seemed like they'd popped out at a clearing in the surrounding woods. Percy had never jumped out of the building before. The thought of it made him nervous. "What time are we?" he asked.

"I'm not sure. This wasn't plotted out yet." Harold turned to examine Percy with quick, beady eyes. "Golly, I sure do have some questions for you. But we should get somewhere safe until we figure out when we are."

Percy nodded, and the two boys climbed to their feet. The air was tight, and the sun felt heavy on Percy's skin, letting him know it was late summer. He followed Harold as he guided them further into the forest, navigating over fallen trees and billowing plant growth. Though Percy towered over him, Harold walked like he was at least ten feet tall. Percy wasn't sure why, but he liked Harold. He felt he could trust him. It was the opposite of how he felt when he met Ms. Lisette. There was something about his frankness that put Percy at ease. Besides, what choice did he have? If he was ever going to find his way back to Mama, he was going to need his help. Especially now that he lost Mei.

Again, the rumble of a voice. Percy looked up from his feet to see an old shack not far from where they walked. Harold spun around so Percy could see his mouth move. "It was left behind when the hotel was built," he explained. "Some old man lived here, trying to harness the power of the springs. Not many know about it but me."

As they grew closer, Percy noted the brush and heavy moss that covered the logs. It looked as if someone had intentionally camouflaged it. Nearby, a small stream ran over little hills of rocks.

Harold ran forward and shoved the door open, releasing a plume of natural dust into the air. Percy was surprised to see the shack had been maintained. Though it was only one room, there was enough space for a bed, dresser, and chest, with a table and chair near an old stone fireplace. Rusted kitchen equipment hung on the walls. From the looks of the shack, at least, it seemed Percy and Harold were still in the old days.

Harold went over to the chest and flipped it open, revealing dozens of old books and papers. Percy noticed bundles of paper money, printed in different ways.

Harold shuffled through everything before finding what he was looking for. "Ah, here it is." He brandished an old, leather-bound journal. Etched on the front was the word *Meadowbrook*. "This is my journal," he explained, "gifted to me by my adult self."

Percy's eyes widened.

"This is how I know everything about everything about time-hopping, or 'jumping,' as you call it. What portals to use to get to what year, the rules... my adult self wrote it all in here." Harold's eyes shone behind the lenses of his glasses. "One day, I own the hotel, Percy. And now that I've met you, you can come along with me. A man needs all the friends he can get, especially ones that already know about time-hopping. I don't think a lot of folks would be too keen about that."

Percy frowned, letting Harold's words sink in. Finally, he asked, "Do you know my mother?"

Harold brightened. "Ah! We can check the timeline." He turned through the pages. Percy noticed they were all filled with ink, along with several pages dedicated to charcoal sketches and others bearing strange, intricate designs.

Harold finally spoke. "It looks like I met a lady named June in 1954, but she disappeared shortly after. Old Me believes she time-hopped. Her husband followed her."

Percy couldn't help himself; he grabbed the journal.

Met a lovely couple this afternoon, a Percy and June Clark. The lady appeared to be two months pregnant and was deeply hesitant. I can only ascertain the hotel brought them here, as she promptly time-hopped not more than an hour after she arrived. Her husband, thinking she had drowned, tried to rescue her and time-hopped himself. I thought to follow them both, but the portal closed for me. I drained the pool and marked it appropriately. I have yet to run into either of them in my travels, but I do wonder if she's the nurse June from 1960. Will explore later.

Harold didn't separate his parents like Lisette said, Percy thought. Then another thought struck him and he threw the journal back at Harold. "We need to find this pool so I can go back!" he signed wildly. "That's how I can get back to Mama!"

Harold paled. "I don't know if we can—Old Me says the portal is closed. Besides...." He showed him the first page of the journal, which read *Harold's Rules for Time-Hopping.*

"Old Me left warnings about the hotel," he said, turning the book back around to read. "The first one is, never try to leave, or you'll be forcibly thrown back. The second is, never travel to a time where you existed if you can avoid it. If you run into yourself from another time, one of you will abruptly die. You don't know which version."

"But she was pregnant with me—"

"Say the portal does work for you. Do you really want to risk it? What if you kill yourself before you're even born, and you both die?" Harold shivered as if horrified by the thought.

Percy sunk into the chair by the fireplace. The wood creaked with his weight. "I've been alongside her this whole time, so I don't know when it would be safe to try to reunite. It would have to be well after it was a hospital..."

Harold's eyes grew wide. "Oh wow, so you are from the 1960s... Well, I'll be damned. I never met anyone that far in the future before. Well, that I can remember on this timeline, anyway." Harold set the book down and stood to put a reassuring hand on Percy's shoulder. "Don't worry, Percy. We will figure all this out. You and me are in this together."

"So what should we do?"

Harold put up a finger to signal 'one moment,' then dashed back to the trunk. He retrieved a handful of different-sized papers. "These were also left for me. Apparently, they're very important papers saying I'm a professional. They're called degrees—one says I'm a lawyer, another that I'm a doctor... I don't know how, but my adult self left it all for me. He left me tons of books, too, all with instructions."

Percy looked into the trunk; Harold was right. There was a seemingly unending supply featuring some books he'd never seen before. The book lover in him couldn't help but yearn to read them. It was nice to meet someone who liked learning as much as he did.

"I can't jump for a while," Harold continued. "Another rule is that if you constantly time-hop, you don't age. If you stop for a period of time, then your body will. I need to let myself become a grown-up so I can purchase this hotel back at the beginning. I know all this sounds crazy, but I trust what my adult self wrote to me. I need that hotel."

Percy looked away. As much as he liked Harold, he wasn't sure how he'd be able to live with him for years while his mother was still trapped in the hotel.

Harold waved to get his attention. Then he pointed to an old blueprint toward the back of the book, where an old swimming pool had been drawn with a symbol on top of it. It was labeled: *June, 1954, end point unknown.* "This is it! Where she disappeared. It's near the east wing—I know exactly how to get there. Maybe we should chance it..."

Percy brightened. "Let's go!"

"Wait—but we don't know if there even is a pool. We could be so far in the past that it doesn't exist."

"Then we need to find out what year it is."

Harold looked nervous. "I'm scared to go near the hotel, Percy. There's a reason we popped out here."

"Call me P.J. That's what my mama called me."

"Okay, P.J.," Harold said, "I have another idea. We wait until the sun sets, and then we creep close to the hotel. If anyone is in there, they'll be sound asleep. We just gotta pray we don't see ourselves out the window, or something like that."

"You stay behind," Percy suggested. "I'll find out if I can use the pool on my own."

"But what if that mob is still in there searching for you? We might have only hopped a few days."

Percy thought for a moment, remembering his conversation with Lisette. "Still, if *you* die, who knows what will happen? What if you never end up buying the hotel? I'll tell you what—we sneak there together. Then you hang back while I go to the pool. If the portal is closed, I join back up with you and we come back here. If it works..." He trailed off.

Harold caught his drift. "I'm quite sure with all these diagrams, I'll be able to find you again," he assured him. "Then we can learn what's in all these books together."

Percy smiled. "Deal."

Harold jumped up to stash his things away. "Now there is one more thing we gotta do to make sure the hotel is happy."

Percy stared at him, wondering if he'd signed the right thing. "What do you mean?" he asked.

"Don't worry, I'll take care of it," Harold said dismissively. "You just hang out here for a bit. I'll be back well before sundown."

Panic settled over Percy, but he pushed it aside and nodded.

Harold left with a cheerful smile and wave.

Percy settled onto the old bed, which promptly exhaled a cloud of pollen. He coughed, waving the particles from his face. Alone with his thoughts, he recalled his conversation with Lisette. He was fully convinced she was the crazy one, even if she did rescue Mei. Maybe it was all some misunderstanding. He'd seen his father, and now the important thing was that he reunited with Mama.

I guess now I wait...

———

An orange glow had settled around the shack when Harold returned. He was covered in sweat and panting, with streaks of blood on his shirt and hands.

Percy sprang to his feet in alarm. "What happened?"

"Don't you worry about that, P.J., ol' boy," Harold said breathlessly. He peeled off his stained shirt, knowing exactly where to retrieve another one—albeit much larger. He hurriedly tucked the loose ends into his trousers. "Are you ready to go? We don't have much time—it's better to leave now while there's a little light so we won't be stumbling over branches in the dark, making a racket."

Percy nodded, though he felt unsettled. Still, he was eager to get moving. He followed Harold out the door, leaving the shack behind. Humidity clogged the air, and Percy thought it smelled like rain. He wondered if this would work and if he'd ever see Harold again. He knew trying to jump alone was foolish, but he had to *try*.

Harold slowed his steps so he could sign to him. "I just thought of something. If your mom was pregnant with you when she time-hopped, that means you were born at the hotel."

"You weren't?"

"Not exactly," Harold said cryptically. "The hotel birthed me too, but in her own way, which means you are my brother."

"I always wanted a brother," Percy admitted, liking the sound of it. "The only other kid I met my age was Mei, but I didn't get a chance to know her."

"Mei?"

The sun disappeared behind the treeline, leaving behind pink and orange streaks in the sky. It was only a matter of time before it was too dark for them to communicate.

"She was a patient at the hotel," Percy explained. "She was who I was with when I jumped."

Harold stopped in his tracks. "You mean there is another person trapped in the hotel?"

Percy grew nervous. "Oh, um, I'm not sure. We got separated... I was trying to look for my dad."

Harold frowned. "There was no mention of a girl named Mei or your father after his disappearance in the journal. That means Adult Me never found them."

"Wait, does that mean Adult You told you to look for me?"

A distant rumble of thunder shook the trees.

"We better hurry."

The boys broke through the forest to the meadows, where they began to jog. After a few moments, Percy saw the spires come into view. He'd never seen the hotel from so far away, and he had to admit, it looked pretty scary. They grew closer, and Percy found himself thankful the sky still had stars and a slip of moon preventing total darkness because the hotel was pitch black. Not even a dim light shone throughout the massive building. It towered over them like a shadowy giant with hundreds of black eyes preparing to swallow them whole. Percy shivered.

"It's 1910," Harold signed to him. "The hotel is abandoned."

Percy's stomach sank.

"We're in luck. The pool was dug in 1905, behind the east wing. Follow me."

There was another vibration, this time a big one. Lightning flashed soon after, illuminating Harold's concerned face. It was only a matter of time before the storm clouds reached them, bringing along the downpour.

The boys sprinted through the overgrown grass to the back of the building. Percy felt just as scared as Harold had looked, but he needed to get to her. He couldn't let his fear get the best of him. Who knows how long it had been to her since he left? She'd spend her days worried sick. *And besides,* he thought grimly. *I gotta tell her Daddy was murdered looking for us...*

There was another rumble, then a flash, then the skies opened. Percy could barely see as Harold ducked for cover under the hotel's porch. But Percy carried on. No longer able to communicate, he hoped Harold would know what he was doing and follow their plan.

He squinted like hell in the rain, trying to pick out any shape that looked like a pool. The rain had other plans, heavy droplets that smacked his head and obscured his vision. He tried wiping it away, but it was too much. He started to feel defeated until a bolt of lightning struck too close to where he stood. The quick flash illuminated four ghostly white figures standing at each corner of a dark and now churning pool. Hoping they were old sculptures, and not actual spirits come to see to his demise, he ran forward.

Percy couldn't think. If he thought, he would hesitate.

Instead, he imagined himself running into Mama's arms as he catapulted himself into the dark, icy water, and sank like a stone. This water was not rancid, it was sludge, smothering him immediately. The horrible sense that he had been wrong settled over him. This was not a time-jump after all, this was just the way that he died. Although he knew there was no air in his sludge-choked tomb, his mouth instinctively opened to scream, his heart racing and his legs battling the sludge until he felt them. Arms.

Frantically, he tried to grab them back, sensing—*knowing*—they were hers. But the arms were slippery, almost incorporeal, and as quickly as they had found him, they were gone. Percy didn't have time to grieve, however, for a new sensation gripped him. Slithering, twisting things that coiled around his arms and legs. This time, he didn't scream. They wound themselves around him and pulled, and in an instant, his entire world disappeared.

CHAPTER TEN

Lisette, 1889

Lisette hated her younger sister.

She hid it well, however, wearing her blank, smiling mask as Cordelia's ladies' maids buzzed around her. Cordelia didn't even notice Lisette in the room, admiring her lithe frame in the full-length mirror as her corset strings were tightened and her skirts were draped and pinned. A few tendrils of golden hair grazed her neckline, complimenting the soft pink of her gown. Lisette kept her jealousy at bay, imagining the corset strings wrapped around her neck.

"Tea, madam?"

Lisette looked up to see her sister's butler, who'd accompanied them on their trip to the hotel. Though she tried to soften her voice, her "No, thank you" was heard across the room.

"My dear sister," Cordelia exclaimed with the overexaggerated joy that made men follow her around like she was made of candy. "I did not see you there."

"I slipped in while you were preoccupied," Lisette said with a forced smile. She stepped back to admire her dress. "Is that the latest from Worth's?"

Her sister beamed, running her hands down her basque bodice.

"Oh, but of course. Only the finest for tonight. This is our first appearance since the wedding."

"And where is Mr. Morgan?"

"He should be arriving any moment," she informed her. "You know how our men are with business."

Lisette didn't respond, her forced smile pressing itself into a line. As the eldest daughter of one of the wealthiest men in the United States, Lisette should have had the finest suitors a woman could ask for. Instead, she had been promised to Ernest Morgan, a rich but decrepit old badger that smelled of cigars and fish. Thankfully, he promptly died of old age before the wedding could even take place.

Lisette fared better with her second fiancé, a young and quickly rising business tycoon until he was found dead in his study of apparent alcohol poisoning. By this time, Cordelia had blossomed into womanhood, taking their father's attention completely away from Lisette, leaving her a widow of two deceased fiancées... without a proper widow's fortune.

Cordelia suddenly realized her slight and softened. "I am sorry to speak of such things after your recent loss."

"Please. I barely knew Mr. Morgan or Mr. Vandelle. Their presence is far from missed. You are the wife of one of the richest men in America. You do well to enjoy it."

Cordelia squeezed her hands. "You will have your husband one day, dear sister. And if not, you can always come live with me. I plan on having a full brood of children you can help me raise. Think of how wonderful that would be!"

Lisette struggled not to clamp down on her sister's hands, longing to press her fingernails into her skin until she bled. "You have quite a generous heart, dear sister."

"Ms. Lisette?"

Lisette looked up to see her new ladies' maid, Lucille Scott, standing at the door. "You're ready to be fitted."

Lisette took leave of her sister without another word, grateful for the excuse to head back to her own quarters.

Though the Hawthornes now owned the hotel, her father had a special two-floor suite built for them at the uppermost part of the building. He acted as if the decision was magnanimous, so his special guests could enjoy the first and second-floor chambers. But Lisette knew better. In reality, her father believed upper-level luxury rooms were the way of the future. He'd even had a company from Cleveland drive up to install a specialized ascending room.

The machine made her nervous, but Lisette didn't like to show fear in front of the help. Though Ms. Scott had quickly grown on her since they first were introduced, she didn't like to appear vulnerable to anyone.

They approached the terrible, caged contraption dressed up in shiny gold, and Ms. Scott murmured beside her, "The world seems to be moving so fast."

Though Lisette agreed, she did not reply. She'd barely grown accustomed to the electricity her father insisted upon installing in their Manhattan home and now in the hotel. The ascending room gave her extra pause.

The operator stepped out to welcome them in. "Good afternoon, Ms. Hawthorne. Straight up to your room, then?"

Feeling unsteady on her feet, Lisette immediately sunk into one of the plush cushioned seats, her bustle folding as she sat. "Yes, thank you, Mr. Jenkins."

Ms. Scott climbed over her ruffled skirts to slip in beside her.

Jenkins began to pull and crank until the car groaned and began its lumbering journey upwards. The chandelier swayed in response, violently tossing light across the mirrored walls. Lisette found her reflection, a scowling visage of angry blue eyes and raven hair beside a plain, doe-eyed, and mouse-haired Ms. Scott.

"I have not yet told the ladies about your clothing change," Ms. Scott informed her.

Lisette smirked. "I'm rather looking forward to their faces when they learn of it."

"I'm sure tonight's guests will mirror their reactions."

"Good," Lisette said. "Cordelia deserves to be upstaged."

She found her reflection once more, recalling the last time she'd been a guest at Meadowbrook Estates Grand Hotel. It had been almost a year ago, on the night her dear sister's betrothal had been announced. Her father had just purchased the hotel and wanted an excuse to bring the most distinguished guests to show off his new investment. It was a gala unlike any other; all of high society, and its rich hopefuls, were in attendance. Even the former U.S. Congressman James G. Blaine made the trip.

Lisette, fully swathed in mourning attire, had walked in with her head proudly held high. She was still a Hawthorne, after all, regardless of the rumors that swirled around about her. She'd kept it high even as her father made his grand announcement, "I would like to formally announce the betrothal of my daughter, Cordelia Hawthorn, to Mr. James Ashton."

As the crowd erupted into applause, Lisette struggled to keep her face impassive. The Ashton family was one of the wealthiest families in the country with ties to royalty. Their marriage would grant her sister and her children a fortune far greater than that of even the Hawthornes. Cordelia had not only stolen Lisette's attention from their father, but she now had the full attention of all members of high society.

It was at that moment, that she met Harold.

"Do not fret, Ms. Hawthorne."

She had whipped around to see her father's lawyer, her face a mask of fury. Remarkably, he did not falter. Instead, he met her with unwavering gray eyes hidden behind the lenses of his wire-rimmed spectacles. Though he dressed well, he looked out of place amongst the elite, a few brown curls grazing a too-wide forehead.

"Forgive me," she said through gritted teeth. Guests shuffled past them on their way to congratulate the happy couple. "I am not certain what you mean. I am positively thrilled to learn of my dear sister's betrothal."

"Please allow me the next dance. I have something important to discuss with you. I promise you'll want to hear it."

Lisette had stared at him in wordless fury until the orchestra resumed its gay, upbeat tempo, and the beaming couple led the crowd in a waltz. Harold put his hands on her waist and whisked her away from the platform where she had stood. They fell into sync with the others, swirling around the room as Lisette forced him to keep bodily distance from her. With all the whispers swirling around her name, the last thing she wanted was to be accused of entertaining yet another fiancé, especially one far beneath her class.

"Thank you for allowing me this dance," Harold tried. "It means the world to me."

Though she tried to keep her face pleasant, she couldn't help but let out a snort. "Did I have a choice?"

He laughed nervously, taken aback. "That was not my intent. I figured the infamous 'Black Widow' would appreciate being asked to dance by an eligible bachelor."

Hearing her detested moniker spoken aloud instead of behind her back sent a jolt of rage throughout her body. She squeezed his hand, pressing her nails into his skin. "How dare you," she hissed.

Nervous sweat beaded on his forehead. "Please, I meant no offense. I-I am not the best at conversing with such a beautiful woman."

"Conversations are not meant to be had when dancing."

"Well, yes, but I needed to speak to you alone without raising suspicion."

She raised an eyebrow.

"I have a plan to ensure you are richer than your sister."

Lisette stopped mid-dance, nearly colliding with another couple. "Explain yourself this instant," she demanded.

Harold stammered an apology to the couple and pulled Lisette aside. "It is all very complicated." He spoke quickly, his voice lowering to a whisper. "You must trust me. I have been your father's lawyer for years—I have full access to his business records and finances. I know how to make you the richest woman in America."

Lisette found his eyes behind the thick glass. A bold sincerity shone through, but she knew better than to trust anything a man said to her. "And in return?"

"You let me have this hotel."

She let out an incredulous laugh. "That is all?"

"Yes, that is all. This hotel...means something to me. You will inherit it, as well as a vast fortune, but I want the hotel for my own. All you have to do is say yes, and you will surpass even the wealth of your sister. I give you my word."

Back in the present, the shuddering ascending room jolted her back to reality as it settled onto the platform. Lisette blinked, and the vision of her and Harold's conversation faded.

"Are you alright, Ms. Lisette?"

"I am fine." Lisette rose shakily to her feet, assisted by Ms. Scott.

Jenkins hurried to wrench open the gate, then grabbed her arm to steady her. "Careful now, miss."

The smell of his hair reached her nose, and for a fleeting moment, she wondered what it would be like to sleep with a man like Jenkins. She long enjoyed the occasional secret romp with the help, but it'd been long since she felt up to it. Her eyes on him must have caused him apprehension, for he chuckled nervously as he guided her across the elevator platform and into her private parlor.

"Thank you, Jenkins," she said lightly, trying not to giggle at his awkwardness. Oh yes, she would enjoy him very much.

He fumbled back to the elevator as Ms. Scott joined her. If the ladies' maid noticed the interaction, she didn't show it. Instead, she moved forward to push the door to Lisette's chambers open. Inside her gold and marble rooms, a swarm of maids preparing for her fitting.

"Put that away," Lisette immediately snapped to a girl carrying her black lace gown.

Ms. Scott hurried to diffuse the situation. "Ms. Hawthorne has decided to go with a different gown," she told the confused maid. "I will take care of everything. You can start on her hair."

After a warm bath and an hour of poking and prodding, Lisette stood still, admiring herself in her gilded mirror. She smiled, imagining what thoughts ran behind the maids' worried eyes. It wasn't that the dress Lisette had specially delivered from House of Worth was that outrageous, though it did bear intricate details like glass beading, metallic threads, and elephant sleeves. It was because society required Lisette remain in mourning for at least a few more weeks, but instead of donning an appropriate black gown, she would enter the gala drenched in a scandalous shade of cream.

Lisette admired how the low neckline displayed more than just the tops of her ample bosom, her pinned hair revealing her slender neck and collarbones. The Black Widow was dead, she thought triumphantly. She would emerge a butterfly.

"You look radiant, madam." Ms. Scott handed her her silk gloves.

"Why thank you, Ms. Scott," Lisette said. "I will take the stairs down to the ballroom." Though she would have loved to see Jenkins's reaction to her dress, she had no desire to re-enter the blasted ascending room.

By the time Lisette navigated her way down the main stairwell to the grand ballroom, the gala was in full swing. She took her time descending, letting the train of her gown slip down the staircase, one stair at a time, like a satin waterfall. Lisette felt the eyes of all who matriculated in the lobby on her, and she smiled triumphantly.

When her slippered foot reached the ground, the bellman rushed to take her arm. She was pleased to see she made another man visibly flustered.

"I hardly recognized you without your black attire, madame," he stammered.

"The time for mourning has passed, Mr. Delby," she said. "Please proceed."

Though the glittering ballroom was filled with ladies and debutantes in oversized gowns and tuxedo-clad gentlemen, she could pick out the individual clusters, including one with her sister and Mr. Ashton, surrounded by their friends. Her father had his own corner, surrounded by his fellow silver-haired businessmen. That was where she spotted Harold lingering nearby. He was waiting for her.

The clamor of the crowd quieted to a low hum as the bellman led Lisette through the front doors. "Miss Lisette Hawthorne," he announced in a booming voice.

Even with all the people turned to see her, her father's face stuck out. His expression twisted into a quick flash of horror before he forced a smile. She helped herself to a glass of champagne and marched towards him, the details of her dress sparkling under a dozen chandeliers.

"Good evening, Father." She kissed his cheek in greeting.

"I assume you all know my eldest daughter, Lisette," he said to those gathered around him.

"You look lovely, Ms. Lisette," Mrs. Dalton, the wife of her father's partner, said. "My, how time has passed. I did not think your mourning period had ended."

"Quite," Listette said before her father could comment. "I am thrilled to be a part of tonight's festivities."

"I share your jubilation, Ms. Hawthorne," Mr. Dalton said. "Your father has undertaken quite the feat bringing all us city folk up to this mountain."

Her father laughed. "Mark my words, Dalton. This will soon become a lavish retreat unlike any other. It will draw in the crowds."

Lisette noticed Harold behind him, but she did not meet his eyes.

An attendant approached her father. "Sir, it is time for your speech."

Her father nodded and handed off his drink. Without a second look at Lisette, he headed toward the stage where the orchestra played. Lisette smiled. She'd gotten to him.

"Have you given thought to my proposal?" Harold asked, slipping beside her.

"I have," she said, smiling behind her champagne.

"You are glowing," he said, admiring her. "I'm hoping that means you're in agreement."

Lisette slid him a look. "Yes, I agree to your proposal."

A grin erupted across his face. For a moment, in the dim electric light, he seemed almost handsome. He hurried to produce a slip of paper from his pocket and pressed it into her palm. "Here are all of your instructions. I have taken the liberty of instructing Ms. Scott as well."

Taken aback, she turned to study him. "Ms. Scott? What does she have to do—"

They were interrupted by the sound of her father's voice as he spoke loudly into the crowd. "Welcome, all to Meadowbook Estates's 2nd Annual Gala. I have invited you all to join me at this exquisite hotel for some exciting news. It is my great pleasure to announce the next phase of Meadowbrook's development—"

"Ms. Scott will help ensure you arrive tonight as planned," Harold told her in a low voice.

"—known for its miracle spring waters—"

"Tonight? But what of the gala?"

"—baths like the Ancient Romans—"

"We have to move quietly under the cloak of nightfall."

"—glorious gilded fountains—"

"You must trust me, Lisette," Harold whispered. "Soon, you will be the richest woman who ever lived."

"To Meadowbook!" her father yelled.

"I will be there."

"To Meadowbook!" the crowd replied.

———

Frost blanketed the grass, giving the grounds a dewy glow under the moon. Lisette pulled her fur cloak tighter as she walked, annoyed that she was out at such a late hour. Ms. Scott hadn't given her any more information, simply relaying the instructions Harold had given her. "Just a little further, madam."

Lisette saw a small stone chapel peeking out from behind the barren trees. Her breath made plumes of vapor as she surveyed the tiny building, noting candlelight glowing behind the stained glass windows like ominous multi-colored eyes. "He wishes to meet me at a chapel?"

"I suppose so, ma'am."

Lisette signed, hitching up her skirts to ascend the narrow steps. She heard a low hum of voices behind the door, growing silent as Ms. Scott moved forward to push it open. The chapel held two figures standing near a modest cross and unimpressive altar, and as Lisette moved closer, she realized one was a priest. Confused, she looked at Harold, the other figure, who beamed at the sight of her. She stopped in her tracks. "What is the meaning of this?" she demanded.

Harold's face fell as he rushed toward her. "It's part of the plan, my dear."

"A marriage? To *you?*" she sneered.

Harold spoke quickly as if sensing she'd flee. "I promised to make you the richest woman in the country and this is the first step. You must continue to trust me, as you did before. The paperwork has already been drawn up and signed by Father Bellows. The moment we speak our vows, as witnessed by Ms. Scott, the world will be ours."

Nothing he said could calm her rising fury. "I will not submit to a man like you," she insisted. "You are beneath me in all ways."

He suddenly fell to his knees, grabbing her hands to gaze up at her. "You will always have control. The hotel, the money—it is all yours. I only want the hotel, remember? We will only be wed in name; you will have something that no other woman of your status has—autonomy."

Lisette frowned, searching his eyes. There was darkness there, but something more. Ambition, propelled by desperate honesty. She thought of her father, and the smug smile stretched across her sister's lips.

She heard Ms. Scott whisper, "You should trust him, Ms. Lisette."

"Fine."

His smile took on new proportions as he stood and took her hand. "Father Bellows is an old friend of mine," he told her, gesturing to the decrepit priest behind him with sallow skin and a tobacco-stained beard. He wore a look about him that resembled a caged animal, his vestments aged and tattered.

Lisette looked away in disgust.

The ceremony was brief and painless, though Harold appeared overjoyed at every moment. Lisette could barely listen to his sermon as if lost in a daze. She certainly never believed this would be what her wedding was like, but oddly, its unconventionalism felt like the perfect slight towards her father. Doing something so forbidden under the cloak of nightfall gave her a thrill.

Father Bellows snapped her out of her jubilation with the words, "You may now kiss the bride."

She tried not to grow nauseous as Harold leaned in for a rather sloppy kiss. She held her breath until it was finished. Harold, on the other hand, grinned ear to ear, his face flushed pink beneath his glasses.

Ms. Scott snatched up the papers. "I will make sure this gets filed immediately," she told Harold. Then she started out the door.

Confused, Lisette began to ask who gave her the authority to do such a thing when a scream pierced through the night.

"What in Heaven's name..." Lisette murmured, gathering her cloak around her.

"Heaven have mercy, I think it's fire," Ms. Scott gasped at the door.

Lisette rushed out of the chapel, shoving her away. Angry orange flames burned away at the night sky, illuminating the vision of fleeing figures below. The eastern tower had caught fire. Before anyone could stop her, Lisette gathered up her skirts and raced toward the hotel.

Calamity seized Meadowbrook, swarms of disheveled guests in

nightgowns and housecoats spilling into the night. Lisette pushed past them all, hurrying up the front steps to greet the pandemonium head-on. She froze then, unable to do anything more than stand wide-eyed in the lobby as bodies rushed around, all too consumed by their own terror to think to pull a lady away to safety. Though the eastern tower was far from where she stood, she swore she could feel the heat. She knew it was only a matter of time before the fire roared its way down to consume the entire wing. Then it dawned on her that the only part of the hotel on fire was hers—the new wing built for the elite. She whipped around, searching the faces of the people around her. Most looked like hotel staff. Her father and all his guests were trapped in the flames...

A firm hand gripped her arm. "Madam, we must go."

She whipped around to see the terrified face of Father Bellows.

A strangely calm Harold stood behind him. "He's right, my love. The proper authorities will arrive to put out the flames. We must get you to safety."

"But all my things—"

"They are all waiting for you in my carriage," Harold told her, taking her arm from Bellows. He started to guide her back to the door. "I had Ms. Scott gather your most precious belongings before we spoke our vows. She took care of everything before heading into town."

Something crashed above them, and Harold pulled her away from the shards and debris the impact released. Black smoke began to billow into the lobby from above.

"We must go," Harold warned.

"But—but my sister..."

There was another crash, this one was followed by a weak *ding!*

Lisette realized it was the ascending car. She couldn't help but stare as it fell to the platform directly across from where they stood, the gate wide open to reveal a broken chandelier, shattered mirrors, and a lump of something on the ground.

"My God, no," Father Bellows cried. Then he promptly retched.

It took Lisette a moment to realize what she was seeing.

"Where—where is her head?"

No one spoke or moved to stop her as Lisette approached the elevator car that held the torso of her sister. Blood continued to spill from the hole in her neck where her head had been severed, shards of glass sticking out of her like a pin cushion. She still wore her pink silk gown, but no longer were there any blonde curls to compliment it.

Harold breezed past her into the car and kicked her sister's torso to the side. It landed with a sickening thump. "Must have been an accident when she tried to flee. I've read about elevator decapitations, but we have no time to speculate. This is our sign from the hotel." He grabbed Lisette's hand, but she wrenched it free.

"Are you mad? The entire hotel will soon be aflame!"

A desperate look crossed his face. "Lisette, this is all part of it. You have trusted me thus far—you must continue."

Lisette realized she was shaking. Smoke now choked the entire bottom floor as the hotel crumbled around them. She heard the priest's desperate hacking as several broken beams crashed and tumbled down the stairwell.

Harold kept his hand out impatiently. "Please, Lisette! We must go!"

"Madam, no," Father Bellows suddenly cried out between heaves. Lisette could barely see his silhouette through the thickening smoke. "That man is the devil!"

There was another crash, and part of the ceiling caved in.

"Then I am the devil's wife." Lisette lifted her skirt and stepped into the elevator car with determination. She looked back to see if Father Bellows would flee or follow, and watched as he made a wide-eyed sign of the cross. The rest of the ceiling collapsed around him just as Harold turned the knob. Lisette fell to the floor and the elevator fell with her. She squeezed her eyes shut, fully expecting death to come. *I suppose I will not be a rich woman after all...* She braced for the inevitable impact when the car suddenly slowed.

Her eyes slowly opened as the car came to a gradual, gentle halt.

"Come, look."

She looked up to see Harold smiling above her. She took his extended hand and stood. The elevator car had opened on a fully operational hotel floor. Warm electricity was the only thing flooding the hall, smoldering in strange overhead light fixtures. She could smell new rugs and fresh paint.

Lisette frowned, deeply confused. "Where are we?"

An oddly dressed, older woman appeared from around the corner, accompanied by a tall, broad man with dark skin. "You must be Lisette," the woman said warmly. "Harold has told me so much about you. I am Helen Bartlby, Harry's mother. Welcome to the year 1935."

CHAPTER ELEVEN

Harold, 1865

The boy who would one day be called Harold Dobby knew his pa would kill him the moment his ma died.

The Angel of Death took her one warm spring afternoon, her soul floating away like dandelion seeds. He felt numb, even as his sister hit the floor and dissolved into a puddle of sobs. Harold couldn't afford to do the same. Pa would be coming home soon, reeking of cheap moonshine. Someone had to protect her when he let loose his rage.

Harold felt numb again when his sister died, this time praying the sickness would take him too. But it never came, and neither did the tears, even as Harold dug up two graves in their backyard all by himself. Pa didn't even ask Father Bellows to come say words. Harold made up his own verses.

Pa's mind got worse, even worse than he had expected. Though Harold was now responsible for all the household chores, planting seed, and fixing meals, Pa didn't show an ounce of gratitude. He took all his grief and anger out on him; the beatings he once got a few times a month were now worse than ever. Harold knew it was only a matter of time before he killed him. He needed to escape, but where could he go?

The Meadows, as the townsfolk lovingly referred to Boughton Springs, was a small town in the middle of nowhere. Realizing the protection the mountains offered them, as well as fresh springs, early settlers thought they'd struck gold. But their cozy isolation only lasted so long. About a month before Ma died, a bunch of city men came through, claiming they were building a railroad to bring prosperity into the town. The Meadows folk were hesitant to believe them, but they grew especially suspicious when droves of immigrants came into Boughton to build them.

Hatred grew as what Pa called "the Orientals" came into town to buy provisions. Fortunately, the outsiders maintained a respectful distance otherwise, which kept tensions at bay. But when sickness began spreading through the town, the fragile peace collapsed. The outsiders were an easy source of blame for the disease, though Harold was pretty sure folks got sick like that all the time, especially when the ground thawed. Regardless, half the town fell, as well as all of the children. The crop suffered, and daily life in Boughton Springs quickly fell apart. The last few original Meadows folk were forced to work alongside the outsiders to make ends meet. Suffice it to say, it was not a happy arrangement.

Harold dreamed of stowing away on the train once it became operational, but he knew that even if he did manage to sneak aboard, he'd never been farther than a little town outside the Meadows. In fact, the only thing he knew about the world was from the books Ma had kept hidden from Pa. The books she'd hidden inside Bible covers. The books he buried alongside her in the garden.

Harold made do until the moment the railroad was complete, and the city folk began work on a brand new hotel. Boughton was home to dozens of natural springs, and the city men now wanted to create a place where rich folks could come drink it and be well. They said the springs had magical healing powers, though Harold and the rest of the town knew that nothing about those springs had any healing to them.

When a train car full of whom Pa called "the Irishmen" came into town to build it, Pa finally lost what little control he had left. A stone mason by trade, he was convinced the hotel and its workers would ruin him. Screaming obscenities Harold hadn't even heard before, Pa drunkenly throttled him within an inch of his life.

The thought occurred to Harold, as spots began to form in front of his eyes, that there would be escape for him after all. Death would be his escape.

But when Harold's eyes wrenched back open, it wasn't his ma and sister he saw waiting for him in Heaven. It was cruel, bright sky and the sensation of a rake being drug down his back. He realized he was being dragged by his feet through the meadow. His head throbbed, and he could taste metallic blood sharp in his mouth. He tried to pull himself free but found he couldn't, only able to cry out in pain as his skin snagged on rocks and branches.

"Be still, boy!" came Pa's frantic voice. "I gotta take you to them!"

Harold had never heard such shrillness in Pa's voice before. It scared him more than his anger. He squinted to see around him, mustering up enough energy to dodge the rocks as he was dragged. Just as he was quite sure he would pass out again, Pa dropped him like a sack of flour.

Harold struggled to sit upright, his body shaking from everything it had been forced to endure. A crowd had gathered near the springs. Harold couldn't believe his eyes. Father Bellows, Mayor Clayton, the Hills, Tom the blacksmith, the shopkeep—all stood there, staring. Panic gripped him; he'd been warned as early as he could remember to stay far away from the springs. "Nothing good comes from those waters, boy," Pa used to say. "The Injins put a curse on 'em to kill us good Christian folk." *What were they all doing standing so close? Why weren't they trying to save him from Pa?*

"There, I did my part," Pa said, the shrill pitch still present in his voice.

He was met with kind words and hearty slaps on the back. One of the men Harold recognized from the tavern, Henry Jones, pushed a grimy bottle of shine into his shaking hands. Pa immediately took a swig as a few of the townspeople gathered around him.

"You did good, John. You did good."

"Atta boy, John."

"Don't worry, John. It's just like all those animals gave 'em."

"God will forgive you," Father Bellows offered.

Harold wasn't sure what they meant to do, but he wasn't ready to find out. He flipped onto his stomach and began clawing his way forward.

"He's trying to get away!" a woman cried.

He felt several men grab him, one holding him down while another tied ropes around his feet.

"No, please!"

Harold thrashed wildly, twisting around his captors to learn the ropes being wound around his ankles were also tied around heavy rocks. His panic hit a fever pitch, and he began to scream, the cruel reality that he was about to be drowned slamming into him like an angry fist.

"Gag him!"

One of the men tied a dirty rag around his head and twisted the fabric tight. Harold struggled to breathe through his snotty nose as Henry and his own Pa grabbed the rocks to pull him forward. He heard the crowd murmuring all around him.

"Lord have mercy..."

"Lord, accept our prayers!"

"In Jesus's name..."

Harold could do nothing more than helplessly sob. The men paused at the edge of the springs, and Mayor Clayton stepped forward to quiet the crowd.

He turned, stretching his arms wide over the water. "See us gathered before you, O Ancient Guardians!" he shouted. Father Bellows began to pray quietly nearby, making the sign of the cross over where Harold lay.

"Accept our sacrifice!" Mayor Clayton continued. "Just as Abraham offered his son to the Lord, we offer you our last living child, that his sacrifice will urge you to rid us of all who seek to defile our good, Christian town with wickedness and disease! Take this child of sin so your thirst may be quenched, and God can come back to our home!"

"Praise Jesus!"

"Deliver us!"

Harold was pulled forward again as the crowd began to chant. It was nothing like the prayers he'd heard in church. It was a strange, foreign sound that filled Harold with dread. Fortunately, unconsciousness threatened to take hold, his exhaustion and pain winning over his panic. *Let them take me*, he thought. He was done fighting.

The thought occurred to him to pray, but he'd lost his faith long ago. Seemed like if there really was some all-powerful being in the sky, he sure didn't care about Harold. Instead, he prayed to his ma, imagining her as the water hit his feet and he felt himself sinking downward.

"Deliver us, oh ancient ones! Deliver us!"

Please let it be over quick, Ma. I'm so tired.

Strangely enough, as Harold began his rapid descent, he could still hear the crowd chanting so loud it felt like they were right in his ear. Their voices turned low and deep, almost as though the earth itself rumbled. Harold waited to hit the bottom of the springs, but he kept sinking further and further as the water grew colder with each heartbeat. His eyes burst open, surprised to find it hadn't gotten any darker as he sank. The water stayed light as if he bobbed at the surface under the sun.

The deep, rumbling voices never left his ears, and it made him wonder if it was just part of dying. *I never thought about drowning before,* he thought miserably. He would have put money on his death coming with one sharp kick to the head.

His lungs burned from holding his breath, and suddenly, a burst of exhilaration seized him. Maybe he still had time to free his feet and rise to the surface. The crowd would have left by now. But even with the jolt of energy, his weak fingers were no match for the knots around his ankles. The struggle hurt his lungs even more, and he relented, the heavy rocks continuing their sadistic downward pull, which seemed to have no end. Harold started to see spots again as his body begged for air. He wished the sinking would stop; there was no way the springs could be so deep—*when would he stop falling?*

Then he saw them.

Grotesquely long, giant faces surrounded him, solemnly watching his descent. Like sculptures of mountainous rock, their hollow eyes bore into him, like open mouths waiting for a meal. Harold knew he was dying then because he realized it was this chorus of watery giants who chanted in his ears, waiting for his demise. They bent and loomed over him as he sank past them, grinning and grimacing as he descended.

Harold finally screamed, a muted, bubbling scream, squeezing his eyes shut as he thrashed. But when his lungs tried to re-inflate, it was not water that filled them, but air. He opened his eyes again to find he was now submerged in darkness. With a start, he found he was moving up now, no longer sinking down. In fact, he had made it to the water's surface, able to push his mouth out enough to gasp for air. A hard surface prevented him from lifting his head fully out; though he was utterly confused, he didn't question it, sucking in big gulps of precious air. Once his sanity returned, so did his thoughts. He was bobbing now, somehow free of the rocks that had pulled him down.

He reached up to hit the hard surface, realizing it was a plank of wood. He barely had the energy to bob at the surface, and he knew he wouldn't last too much longer. Suddenly, he spotted an opening that let a slip of light through. He swam towards it, and with as much strength as he could muster, he pushed it. Remarkably, the two pieces of wood shifted to widen the opening.

Harold climbed out and lay, panting.

After a few moments, his vision adjusted.

He was in some sort of underground dwelling, and he had just pulled himself out of a pool. He shivered, for the air was cold, and he had still been wearing his warm weather clothes. He looked down at his feet and saw the bruising. It hadn't been a dream. He had really been drowned by his own Pa and the folks he saw every day. The ones he grew up with.

Anger burned in his belly. He didn't know how he was still alive or how he got to this strange place, but he knew he'd find a way to get his revenge.

Ms. Helen, whom he now lovingly referred to in his mind as "Second Ma," wore worry tight across her features. Harold couldn't blame her; he knew how crazy he sounded.

"What do you mean you're going to leave?" she repeated.

"It won't be for too long. Longer than normal, but still." He hoped it wasn't a lie. He'd mapped everything out perfectly. According to his calculations, Second Ma wouldn't miss him for more than a day. "I have it timed just right, so you'll barely even miss me," he promised.

They were interrupted by a quick knock at the door. It was Lucy, right on schedule. "Sister Rose would like to speak to you," she told Second Ma. "I'll look after Harry."

After lingering goodbyes, Second Ma was off, and Lucy and Harold stood alone in her suite, staring at each other.

"Are you sure you're ready for this?" he asked her.

Lucy nodded. Though she was at least ten years older than him, there was something about Lucy that made her seem much younger. Perhaps it was her mind, stunted by the years of abuse she had to endure as a child. It was reflected in her empty doe eyes.

"I'm ready, Harry," she promised.

Harold grabbed his makeshift pack and took her by the hand. Quietly, the two crept out of the dormitory and into the main hall. There was only one way to make it to the basement, and Harold felt nervous every time he had to enter them. He called them "the Tunnels"—a labyrinth of secret passageways that joined each room in the east wing all the way to the lowest floor. He discovered them last year and hadn't told a soul but Lucy; she explained that lots of ritzy places built passageways so servants could move around the floors undetected. Harry couldn't imagine a world where you'd want to block out the people serving you. There was a lot he didn't understand about rich folks. But he would figure it out soon enough. First, he had business to attend to.

The boarded-up pools in the basement had not changed since Harold had emerged from them a year ago. The split board had been completely removed in anticipation of their travels. He searched Lucy's face to gauge her reaction, but she seemed as aloof as ever. When he'd originally told her his plan, she'd given him the same sort of reaction. "I put my newborn baby in the water to free her," she'd said. "I know how this place works."

Harold guided her to the edge of the open pool. He paused to stash his notebook and glasses in his pack, tightening the cords so it was secure. He didn't want to lose anything during their travels, and the pack was his best bet. He even double-wrapped his journal so the pages wouldn't get too wet.

When that was finished, he navigated his way with blurry vision to the rocks he had left in the corner, already wound up in rope. Nausea gripped him as he knelt to tie the one to Lucy's ankle, then another on his own. *This is why,* he reminded himself. *This is why we're doing this. Because you still feel sick over it all.*

He stood, retrieving from his pocket a piece of oil pastel he'd stolen from the art room.

Lucy closed her eyes as he drew the precious symbol on her forehead, the one he found etched into the split wooden plank where he'd emerged. He didn't understand it fully, but instinct told him it was important. He made note of it in his journal, along with the other symbols he found and created around the hotel.

Lucy took the pastel from him and drew the symbol on his forehead. As she finished, a rush of excitement hit him then, fueling him to continue unafraid. He tossed the pastel aside, then pulled out a last slip rope from his pack, which he held up to Lucy. "We can't let go of each other's hands, or we might end up in different places. We need to bind our hands together."

Lucy gave another nod and helped him twist the rope until their hands were locked in place.

When they were finally finished, Harold looked down at the murky water below, their distorted reflections peering back. One day, he would come back and clean these pools up, he decided. He never wanted to see dark water again.

"Ready?" On her nod, Harold took a deep, shuddering breath as he gripped Lucy's hand as tight as he could. "O Ancient Guardians," he whispered. "Take me back to where I need to be."

On a three count, they jumped.

This time, it moved much faster.

Before Harold could even look for The Guardians, he and Lucy burst out of the water, finding themselves in the middle of the springs. She gasped for air, obviously rattled, but Harold kept his grip on her, helping her swim to the edge. As soon as they launched themselves onto the grassy bank, Lucy sputtered, "Did we make it? Are we here?"

Breathless, Harold looked around. The shrill crickets and warm setting sun let him know it was summer, and he recognized the Meadows. But what year it was, he was unclear. Though he had a hunch they'd be transported to 1865 again, the time was always determined by the hotel. That was one certainty no one could argue with.

They quickly unwound their hands and ankles and stood.

"It's so peaceful," Lucy remarked.

"Yeah," Harold murmured. "Follow me."

They trudged through the tall grass, and Harold tried not to remember his father pulling him through it. Though it had only been a year, it felt like it truly was fifty years ago. He felt so much older now; the knowledge he'd gained from the school library and the hidden books in the hotel had given him an entirely new perspective on life. He felt wiser.

The old church bell tower peeked over the horizon, and soon

the town came into view. Though he tried to prepare himself, Harold stopped dead in his tracks. They'd made it right back to 1865 when he was drowned. He knew this because they had just hung a brand new bell purchased by railroad construction profits. They'd planned to rebuild the whole church the following year. The town of Boughton was still there, just as he left it. All of Harold's prior determination was lost.

Lucy sensed his fear and slid her hand into his. "It's okay, Harry. You can do this. I know you can."

Harold shivered. "We stick to the plan. It's almost nightfall. I will break into the General Store, and you will go to the church. You still think you can handle Father Bellows on your own? It is imperative he comes with us."

"I will take him to the dark place and wait for you to follow."

With a final nod, they took leave of each other. Harold perched behind a shed near the General Store until the sun disappeared from the sky. Old Man Beechum was a drunkard like his father, already headed home to drink his supper; Harold popped open the back door of the shop without issue. It wasn't even locked. He quickly gathered his supplies and slipped out, hoping Lucy had held up her end of the bargain.

When he arrived at the old church, he smiled. The back door was left open, letting him know she'd successfully kidnapped the dastardly priest by knifepoint. Though he had to hammer gently, lest he make noise, it took Harold less than an hour to secure the building. Although the church was far back enough from the town, he didn't want to risk anyone seeing or hearing him.

He paused to wipe the sweat from his brow and hurried to make himself a torch. Then he moved to the bell tower, finding the rope easily and giving it a hard pull.

The church bell clanged, disturbing the peace of the summer evening. He grabbed his makeshift torch and set it aflame, waiting until the lamps were lit and townspeople in nightclothes drifted out of their homes. He walked out of the church, stepping onto the front porch to greet the gathering crowd head-on. His torch burned brightly in his hand, empowering him like the clang of the bells.

Murmurations of fear, awe, and amazement rolled through the crowd as they grew closer, one woman letting loose a shriek of recognition. But before they could panic, Harold cleared his throat and spoke. "Your eyes do not deceive you," he cried out. "It is I, the prodigal son of John Edwards Dobby. The Guardians have spared me!"

Several fell to their knees, humbled by their fear.

"I have come to take what is owed to me!" He pointed at the crowd. "Bring me my father, and your lives will be spared."

Without hesitation, they parted, and a few men Harold couldn't recognize from afar shoved his father to the front.

Harold sneered with disgust. Even at a distance, he could tell his father had not bathed in weeks. What cowered before him was nothing but a soiled, pathetic excuse from a man wearing piss-stained trousers and clutching his bottle of moonshine. How had he once been so terrified of something so weak?

"Forgive me, son!" he slurred, tumbling into the dirt. "Forgive me!"

Harold pulled snot into his throat and spat, the mucus landing squarely on his father's cheek.

"You will all enter the church now," Harold commanded. "All except my father."

Hesitant, the townsfolk of Boughton shuffled forward into the church. Fear swam in their eyes, but Harold did not waver. He simply stared, furious and unwavering, as each one entered. Then he called his father forward.

The drunkard could barely make it up the steps. "You gotta forgive me..." he gasped as he reached the top of the stairs.

But Harold did not hesitate. He snatched the bottle from his father's grasp and doused him in its stinking liquid. Then he pushed his lit torch squarely into his chest.

His father burst into flames, immediately letting loose an inhuman scream. Harold shoved him into the church and slammed shut the door. Then, he quickly pulled down the beam he had installed moments before their arrival. Screams rattled against the walls as the church quickly filled with fire. Harold was sure that the beam, plus the bolted windows, would keep anyone from escaping, but he hammered in a few extra nails as he enjoyed the anguished cries from within. When it grew too hot to bear, he retreated, stepping back one last time to admire his handiwork. He watched as desperate, charred limbs tried to escape the inferno from the boards over the windows, only to go limp as their owners were ravaged by fire. Within moments, the screaming ceased, and the entire building was consumed by flame. *It's beautiful,* Harold thought, enjoying the warm glow on his face. Too bad Lucy wasn't there to see it.

He headed back to the springs feeling lighter than he had ever before. He broke into a whistle, looking forward to seeing Lucy. Who knew where things could go from here? One thing was for certain—the Guardians chose him to be their instrument, and Meadowbrook was their tool. In fact, Meadowbrook was his true mother—she had birthed him, after all, and he knew she would guide his path.

He was unstoppable now.

EPILOGUE

Heather, 2019

"Are you recording?"

"Yes, Chad."

Heather hated recording on her phone, but neither one of them had felt like hauling more equipment than needed up the damn mountain. As a way to deter urbexers, the old hotel had been closed off well before its long driveway began. But this was not their first rodeo; they had been exploring abandoned buildings for years.

Chad took position right below the rusted sign over the front gates that read *Meadowbrook*. Then he took a deep breath. "Here we are at the infamous Meadowbrook Hotel, the most haunted hotel in America. In this episode of Ghost Hunters Z, we will explore the decrepit old mansion once called 'A Castle in the Sky.'"

Heather paused the recording and peered down the driveway, overgrown with brush. She tucked her phone into her pack and unsheathed her hiking machete. She led the way, hacking at the overgrown brush to clear a path. Tufts of pollen and tiny bugs flew up around her, angry to be disturbed.

"Looks like we're the first people to come up here this year," Chad said from behind her.

"Maybe the hotel isn't as cool as it used to be."

"Heather, the dude used to tell people he could cure cancer. Pumped them full of watermelon seed juice. Let alone the other stories..."

"I know the lore, Chad. I'm just saying. People get sick of shit quick nowadays."

"Well, our subscribers are gonna love this piece."

The sun hung high in the sky, and Heather's shirt had soaked through with sweat by the time they finally made it to the hotel entrance. It towered above them, cloaking them in blissful shade. She could see into the building from the broken doors, sunlight catching on the broken glass and illuminating the old lobby. She could smell the rotting wood and mildew from where she stood. She smiled; she loved abandoned places. Though her opinion of Chad wasn't exactly favorable, she was grateful for the opportunity to explore them.

"Can we help you?"

Heather whipped around to see a little old Black lady pointing a crooked finger in her direction, her lips pressed into an angry scowl. Behind her stood one of the tallest black men she'd ever seen, also scowling.

"Ain't no need for that weapon, missy."

Confused, Heather remembered the machete in her hand. "Oh my gosh, I'm so sorry. I just brought it for the weeds." She carefully lowered herself into a squat and set the machete on the grass.

Chad pushed forward, unfolding a paper. "We have a permit—"

"I don't care about all that," the old lady snorted. "You kids shouldn't be poking around up here."

Heather looked to the man towering behind her. "Sorry to disturb you. We thought this place was fully abandoned."

"He can't hear you," the lady told her. "He's deaf. We don't set foot in that damned place anymore. There hasn't been anyone in it for years, and it's hungry. We stay in the groundskeeper's house, and that's what we do—take care of the grounds and make sure fools like yourselves don't enter that damn hotel."

The man behind her put a calming hand on her shoulder.

"I don't care anymore, P.J.," she said. "I'm not pretending for the public anymore. That hotel has ruined lives—including ours—and I'm not letting it happen again."

Heather inwardly groaned, knowing her words put dollar signs in Chad's eyes. Sure enough, he took another step forward.

"So you know the history of this place?" he said with feigned innocence. "Do you mind if we interview you?"

The old lady eyeballed the phone in Heather's hand. "I'll talk to you so you won't go in that damned hotel, but I don't want to be recorded."

"Of course not," Chad assured her while gesturing the opposite to Heather. "We just want to know more about this place. Can you tell me your names?"

"Ms. Clark and this is my son, P.J. You have five minutes, then we're headed back for lunch."

"When you say the hotel separated you..."

"This isn't a typical building," Ms. Clark began.

Chad gestured again to Heather. She pretended to press the record button on her phone. The tall man noticed and smiled.

"This place was built on tragedy," Ms. Clark continued. "Like everywhere else in this damned country, folks tried to settle here ages ago, which meant killing the natives that were here first. But they got what was coming to them. Rich men from New York City came in and took over, wanting to use the springs to draw in other rich people with money to burn. They built a railroad to come through here and everything. Some townsfolk rebelled, so they burned their town to the ground."

"Fascinating."

She snorted. "Not surprised you'd say that."

Heather cleared her throat. "Did you know the infamous owner, Harold Dobby?"

The woman's eyes fell on her, growing dark as she spoke. "That man is the Devil, through and through. Don't let my son tell you otherwise."

P.J. shook his head and signed, "He's my friend. Mama hates him."

"He manipulates everything for his own gain," Ms. Clark insisted. "A true narcissist. You walk into that hotel and no matter what time, you end up someplace else. That hotel is evil."

"Manipulates? I thought he died."

P.J. stepped in front of his mother and signed, "We're done here."

Chad began to protest, but Heather interrupted. "Thank you so much for your time."

P.J. nodded and started to guide his mother away.

"We shouldn't let them go in there, P.J.," she hissed, angry to be shuffled off.

But he said nothing, or perhaps he did, but Heather couldn't see. In a few moments, the two had disappeared down the hill.

"Oh my God, that was gold," Chad said with a huge, shit-eating grin. "Spooky ass Black lady and her giant, deaf son still guarding the hotel? You can't make that shit up."

Heather shook her head in disgust. She just wanted to get her footage of the inside and get gone. "Come on, let's go."

"Get a shot of me going up the stairs. I'll give them some more lore."

Heather sighed and began recording.

Chad cleared his throat."Built in 1886, the Meadowbrook Hotel promised a luxurious retreat from everyday life. Wealthy oil tycoon Thomas Hawthorne purchased it in 1888 and installed intricate Roman bath-style pools in its basement. Full of water from the nearby springs, it was said that soaking daily would cure any disease."

They entered the lobby, where remnants of the beautiful restoration project that occurred in the 1990s had fallen into disarray. It was strange to see something that had been abandoned, restored, then abandoned again. Her eyes swept over the tarnished gold and cracking busts of cherubs. H. Higglebottom was the name they found on the restoration paperwork, but he died before the project was complete. He was also listed as the last owner of the hotel. Meadowbrook lore enthusiasts speculated it was actually Harold Dobby.

"Here we see what is left of H. Higglebottom's restoration project," Chad told the camera. "He tried to recapture what the hotel was like during the hotel's peak, when hundreds of patrons flocked to the hotel, including the elite, whom Thomas Hawthorne personally invited to attend lavish balls."

Glass crunched under Heather's feet as they moved into the ballroom, the only place with its windows intact.

"In 1889, Hawthorne threw a party that would be his last. Unlike his colleagues, Hawthorne was not afraid of innovation and had the entire hotel wired for electricity. He also had one of the first elevators installed. Some speculate an electrical fire is the reason why the hotel burst into devastating flames, but whatever the reason, the entire eastern wing was ravaged by fire. Some say you can still see the ghosts of the guests in this very ballroom where we stand." He looked around somberly, then began the cringe acting he always did for episodes. Heather tried not to sigh.

"Did you feel that?" he said in fake terror. "I feel a presence nearby."

"I totally feel it," Heather lied.

"Let's set up some of our equipment here when night falls. I think we'll definitely pick up some paranormal activity here."

Heather nodded.

"Come on, let's go into the east wing where the fountain is."

Suddenly, there was a tiny ding that cut down the hall. Heather froze in her tracks. "Did you hear that?"

For the first time, Chad looked genuinely cornered. "An elevator ding?"

Heather nodded.

"Dude." Chad walked back to the lobby, thoroughly intrigued. "Make sure you're recording this."

Heather hurried to keep up when she suddenly heard Chad cry out in alarm.

"Who the fuck are you?" an angry male voice said.

Heather slowed her walk.

"I-I have a permit," Chad stammered. "We're ghost hunters."

"Ghosts? There ain't no ghosts here, pal. You can keep it moving."

Heather cursed under her breath, wishing she'd brought in her machete. She hadn't anticipated any squatters, but she liked knowing it was near. She wondered if she could dash outside and back in without notice when suddenly a woman's voice chimed behind her.

"Oh, honey, you shouldn't be here."

Heather jumped back. "Who—what—" She could barely focus on the thin blonde woman standing before her over the sounds of a struggle from the other room. The two men had begun to scuffle, but before Heather could react, a scream tore through the silence. It sounded like Chad hurtled down the elevator shaft.

"Sorry about your boyfriend," the woman said over the echoing scream. "Mikey has been really cranky lately. We all are, actually. There's been some kind of hiccup in the timeline and we've all been hopping over and over without stopping for more than a few weeks. It's maddening."

There was a loud splat, and Heather fell to her knees. As much as she hated Chad, thinking of his body smashed at the bottom of an elevator shaft made her sick. "P-please," she begged in terror, shaking so badly she could barely hold her phone.

"Oh, you don't have to worry about me," the woman giggled. "Come on. I know a place to hide."

Unable to do much else, Heather scrambled to her feet and followed the woman up the stairs.

What am I going to do? What am I going to tell everyone back home?

Her mind raced as she hurried to keep up with the woman, who flew up the stairs with an unusually graceful ease. She hoped like hell the other man wouldn't follow. Their ascent was interrupted by another man coming down the other way. Heather held back a scream of alarm.

"Hey, Tommy," the woman greeted him.

"Cindy! You're sure a sight for sore eyes."

The two hugged, and the man's eyes caught sight of Heather, quivering against the wall. "Someone new?"

"I think she's just exploring the hotel. Mikey found her boyfriend, so I'm trying to hide her before he sees her too. Not like he'd hurt a lady, but ya know."

"Yeah, Mikey is a little unpredictable. Especially lately." He turned to address Heather. "Cindy's a good egg—stick by her, and you'll be okay."

"Where you headed?" Cindy asked him.

"Trying to find Lisette. I lost her during the last hop, just as she was telling me she found Helen. That's a good sign, I think."

Cindy sighed. "It's all a fucking mess now, isn't it?"

Tommy shrugged. "I'm sure Harold will figure something out. He always does, that devious bastard. I'll see ya around. Nice meeting you...?

"H-heather," Heather stammered.

What the fuck is going on here?

"Take care, Heather," he said kindly. "I hope, for your sake, I never run into you again." Then he hustled down the stairs.

"Tommy is one of the few good ones," Cindy explained as she resumed her ascent. "Him and Matthew. We used to leave each other notes before we figured out this whole time-hopping thing."

"Time-hopping?"

There was a violent shudder, which threw Cindy against the wall. Heather started to fall backward, but she grabbed the railing before toppling down the stairs. "What the hell is that?" she cried. "New York doesn't get earthquakes!"

Cindy looked sad as another tremor hit moments later. "Sorry, babe, you're in it now with us."

Pieces of the ceiling started to fall, and Heather slid down to the platform, where she folded into a ball.

"Just try to stay sane!" Cindy called over the noise, the building now rattling without pause. It was as if the entire hotel was about to collapse.

More of the ceiling fell, and Heather pushed her head between her legs, shielding herself with her arms. If she could avoid getting crushed, perhaps she could dig her way out. But when she felt the walls cave in, all rational thinking left her body, and she let loose a terrified scream.

And then, all was still.

Surprised to still be alive, Heather peeked out from the rubble. Or what should have been rubble. She was still in the hotel, lying in the middle of the floor, but it was much cleaner. In fact, it was as if it had been restored to the point of operation. Before she could stand to investigate, she noticed a man standing above her wearing an oversized smile. A brightly lit chandelier created a halo behind his head of dark curls, giving him the appearance of being an angel.

"Well, hello there," he said, delight in his voice. "The name is Dobby. Harold Dobby. Welcome to Meadowbrook."

ACKNOWLEDGMENTS

Writing can be a lonely job, but I'm surrounded by so many amazing people. I credit them completely for any book I manage to complete. I still can't believe folks actually like to read what I write, so first and foremost, a huge thank you to the readers who continue to buy my books throughout the years and who support my beloved publishing house.

Speaking of Quill & Crow, to my entire team: Alma, Mel, Kayla, Cyndi, Lisa, the Mat(t)hews, Tiff, and Stef—thank you so very much for not only keeping that machine moving, but for allowing me time to write. Lisa and Matt, thank you for your editing eyeballs. I'm so glad to have found you both. To all the Crows, thank you for all the love and support. The support of the indie community has also been a big part of this book's completion. I am honored to be part of a growing initiative that is changing the face of publishing. Authors supporting authors is a beautiful thing.

And last but not least, my Andrew. Thank you for always believing in me and for faithfully reading everything I write. You were a huge part of this book's inception—from our travels to our long discussions to the creepy woman in the elevator with the too-big smile—and I'm forever grateful for you. And, of course, thank you to my boys for letting Mommy have her writing time. I love you all more than you know.

TRIGGER INDEX

Alcoholism/Addiction
Body Horror (light gore)
Child Abuse (Chp. 11)
Child Death (implied)
Decapitation
Drowning
Medical Abuse
Mental Illness/Abuse (ECT)
Miscarriage (off-screen)
Parent Death (off-screen)
Racism/Sexism
Suicide (attempted)

THANK YOU FOR READING

Thank you for reading *Welcome to Meadowbrook*. We deeply appreciate our readers, and are grateful for everyone who takes the time to leave us a review. If you're interested, please visit our website to find review links. Your reviews help small presses and indie authors thrive, and we appreciate your support.

More Books from Quill & Crow

The Quiet Stillness of Empty Houses, L.V. Russell

There Ought to Be Shadows, Krissie K. Williams

All the Parts of the Soul, Catherine Fearns